# FROGS OUT OF WATER

# Frogs

## OUT OF

# Water

---

*stories*

*by*

# André Malécot

*illustrated by Robert Brandts*

FITHIAN PRESS · SANTA BARBARA, 1998

The stories in this collection originally appeared
in the following publications:

"Doctor Without Borders," *The Iconoclast,* May 1998
"Crevasse," *Jewish Currents,* February 1998
"The Gourmet," *Rafale,* April/May 1992
"The Voice," *The Iconoclast,* August 1996
"Horizons," *The Iconoclast,* August 1997
"A Shade of Difference," *The Short Story Collective,* January 1998
"On the One Paw," *The Short Story Collective,* May 1998
"Why Are They Always Smiling?" *Short Stories Bimonthly,* January 1997
"The Watch," *Rafale,* October/December 1991
"Water for M'Bouka," *The Short Story Collective,* February 1998
"Teddy Bears," *The Best Short Stories,* December 1997
"The Importance of Not Being Ernest," *Atom Mind, May 1998*

Copyright © 1998 by André Malécot
All rights reserved
Printed in the United States of America

Published by Fithian Press
A division of Daniel and Daniel, Publishers, Inc.
Post Office Box 1525
Santa Barbara, CA 93102

Book design: Eric Larson

LIBRARY OF CONGRESS CATALOGING-IN-PUBLICATION DATA
Malécot, André. Frogs out of water : stories / by André Malécot ;
illustrated by Robert Brandts.
p.   cm.
ISBN 1-56474-274-1 (alk. paper)
I. Title.
PS3563.A426F76   1998
813'.54—dc21
98-6692
CIP

*To Dot*

*my wife and severest critic*

# CONTENTS

# FROGS OUT OF WATER

# DOCTOR WITHOUT BORDERS

"HOW many times do I have to spell it out, Monique? Elective surgery on the idle rich is not what I busted my ass in medical school for." Jean-Pierre let go of the patient's wrist and pulled the stethoscope off his neck. "Okay, he's stable. Just keep an eye on him until he wakes up."

She handed him the patient's clipboard. "Can I come over after my shift, sweetheart?"

"Sorry, not tonight. I'm meeting a man from Doctors Without Borders."

"You're really going through with it?"

He gave the data a quick once-over and gestured for something to write with. "I have to. I need a fresh start."

She pulled a ball-point pen from a pocket and handed it to him. "You weren't like this before the Gulf War."

He scribbled a note at the bottom of the chart, initialed it, and handed it back. "In Iraq, I was saving lives. Here, I feel like I'm waiting for Godot."

When he saw her eyes fill with tears, he put the clipboard down and drew her into his arms. Her nurse's cap came up to his chin, and the ethereal scent of her Chanel made him all the more conscious of her vulnerability. "I don't mean to hurt you, *chérie*. I just need to get away and figure out what I want to do with the rest of my life."

"But you know how contagious Ebola is. You can catch it merely by touching a patient. Couldn't you choose someplace else but Africa?"

"It was the only opportunity I could think of."

"Then take me with you. They must need nurses." Her lip was trembling as she turned and shut off the heart monitor.

He hesitated for a moment, then impatiently cuffed the air with a hand and strode out the door. Once in the locker room, he took off his scrubs, and with a frustrated *"Merde!"* hurled them into the dirty-clothes bin. When he removed his surgical cap, his liberated ponytail cascaded down his back. He pulled on his jeans, sweatshirt and sneakers, then grabbed his leather jacket. Before stepping outside, he paused and filled his lungs with the antiseptic air of the hospital, the only thing he liked about Passy, the richest of Paris arrondissements.

In the courtyard, he unchained his vintage Harley-Davidson, caressed the handlebars, and with his handkerchief wiped a smudge off an instrument face. He hopped aboard, gave a little jump, and the machine came to life with a roar. As he sped down the boulevard towards central Paris, weaving in and out of traffic, his mood improved.

At a red light, he pulled up alongside a big Citroën with its windows down. He gunned his engine a couple of times—he loved the sound. The driver, in a business suit, glared at him. "You think you're in Rome, or what?"

Jean-Pierre looked him over and thought, Another stuffed shirt.

He rose from his bike and cast his six-foot-four shadow over the car. After allowing the driver to savor the moment, Jean-Pierre leaned over and rested his forearms on the edge of the window. "Is there a problem?"

The color drained from the man's face. "My apologies, *monsieur*. No offense intended."

The light changed. The Citroën squatted on its haunches, then leaped across the intersection.

Jean-Pierre chuckled and mounted his Harley again.

When he reached the Eighteenth Arrondissement, he swung into the cobblestone courtyard of a drab nineteenth-century apartment house and chained the bike to the railing of the steps to the concierge's door. Then he went around front to the Algerian restaurant on the ground floor.

The waiter grinned widely. "Good evening, Doctor Fouché."

"Good evening, Ahmed."

"The gentleman at the corner table says you're expecting him."

"That's right. Thanks."

As Jean-Pierre approached, the man looked up, surprised. "Doctor Fouché?" Jean-Pierre cultivated the reactions of first timers: This guy is one of the best surgeons in the city? He nodded and held out his hand. "Yes, you are...?"

"Oh, pardon me, I'm Maxime Terrier, at your service. Have you reached a decision?"

"Yes, you can count me in."

"I'm so glad. We heard about your cool-headedness under fire in Iraq. But I must tell you that while this assignment isn't in a war zone, it could be even more life-threatening."

"I know, I've read up on it. So where exactly are you sending me?"

"Mali."

"Mali? I thought the hot zone was farther south."

"It is. We don't know how Ebola skipped up there. Are you sure you don't want a few more days to think it over?"

"No, I'm positive."

"Then it's agreed. I'll leave you to your dinner now. The papers will be in the mail in the morning. *Bon appétit.*"

They shook hands and he left. Ahmed came over with a loaded tray. "Thursday, couscous, right?"

After dinner, Jean-Pierre went up to his room and put on a Mozart piano concerto. He flopped onto his bed and slid his hands behind his head. This was the only music he knew that seemed to be in harmony with the universe and could bring him peace of mind. But there were still traces of Monique's perfume on his pillow—a distraction. He tossed it onto a chair and settled down to think.

Too many problems—Passy, Monique, maybe *me*. Well, Passy certainly isn't the problem—I'll be better off *anywhere* else. Monique? She's good company, intelligent, a sense of humor, devoted, great in bed. But do I love her? Am I capable of loving anybody? Or any deep emotion? Yeah, I did feel something incredible whenever one of the guys I'd patched up in the Gulf War came back to life.

A week later, Jean-Pierre took an Air France flight to Bamako, Mali's capital, then an air-taxi northeastward to Kambilou, a bone-dry town on the Niger River. As the small plane descended over the sand-colored structures and streets, he shook his head. Not a tree, not a bush, not a blade of grass. He wondered how people could live in such a place. As soon as they landed, he climbed into the waiting taxi—an ancient beat-up Peugeot—and asked to be taken to Namba, the village ten kilometers north he'd been assigned to. The driver's eyes opened wide with fear, and Jean-Pierre had to flash a bill in his face. Even then, the man said he'd go only as far as the edge of the village.

Jean-Pierre soon found himself trudging up a dirt road. He stopped a barefoot woman in an ankle-length *boubou* balancing a basket of clothes on her head and asked how to get to the hospital. She pointed at the end of the road and gestured left.

The hospital turned out to be a former tourist enclave consisting of a faded one-story wooden bungalow and half a dozen whitewashed round mud huts with straw roofs. He took the front steps two at a time, dropped his flight bag on the porch, and pushed open the door.

Patients were filing by a table, where a native woman in a nurse's uniform was giving injections to one after the other with a single syringe. When he realized she was only swishing it around in a jar of alcohol between shots, he stepped up to the table and gestured for her to stop. "My God, woman, you're supposed to use a new needle each time."

She looked up. "Who are you?"

"I'm Doctor Fouché."

She shook her head in despair. "I'm sorry, Doctor, I'm doing the best I can. I'm not a nurse, I'm a schoolteacher."

"Who else is there?"

"Two other women from the village. They're not nurses either. Everyone else has fled."

"Where do you keep your syringes?"

"I only have two."

"Don't you sterilize them?"

"I boil them and let them soak in alcohol overnight. Is that all right?"

"What are you inoculating for?"

"Ebola. The doctor we had—before he went crazy and died—made it from the blood of recovered patients. He thought it might work."

Jean-Pierre looked into her eyes, the only part of her face not hidden by her surgical mask. Their golden-brown irises seemed to express unabashed candidness, while the unblemished whites suggested a purity of soul. He realized he was speaking to a person of courage and devotion.

His tone softened. "Okay, but no more inoculations for the moment, please. Where's your Ebola ward?"

"The former dining room is the only ward we have. We assign space on a first-come first-served basis."

"Thanks." He pushed through the line to the rear of the room and opened the door.

The stench of vomit and excrement hit him in the face. He clamped his hand over his nose and mouth and looked around. The floor was filthy with traces of feces and bloodstains. Soiled linen was piled in the corners. Ten dirty beds lined the walls.

Patients were moaning and coughing, and some had blood oozing from their mouth, eyes, nose, and body sores. Viscous black and red smears glistened on one of the walls. A young woman in a soiled uniform, mask and gloves, was pulling a blood-spattered sheet over the face of a corpse. She heard Jean-Pierre and turned. "Get out!"

"I'm the new doctor."

"Oh, thank God!"

"Are these all Ebola patients?"

"No, some have AIDS, some dysentery, others malaria. The rest I can't tell."

A patient at the end of the room began heaving with wrenching groans and throwing up a mixture of blood and a blackish substance. Jean-Pierre instinctively started forward to help. The woman called out, "Don't touch him! He's melting down."

He swore under his breath and retreated. Back in the front room, he suddenly felt a flood of excitement. Yeah, *this* is medicine!

The last of the walk-in patients had left. The woman was cleaning up. She pulled off her surgical mask and gloves and held out her hand. Her beauty took Jean-Pierre by surprise, and he held on for a moment. Her smooth purple-black face was both delicate and sensual, with dazzling white teeth, finely sculptured cheekbones, a slim nose, and lips that evoked fantasies.

She acknowledged his reaction with a smile, then looked him over. He could see she approved.

"Welcome to Namba. I'm sorry about the way I greeted you. I didn't think you were a doctor."

"The ponytail?"

"Partly. Forgive me." She smiled. "My name is Ismaïla."

"Call me Jean-Pierre, please."

"Thank you, but I think we should call you Doctor. It gives people more confidence."

"Whatever you say. Okay, let's get started, things look pretty grim. Tell me, do we have an autoclave?" It had been a long time since he felt this kind of elation.

"It's broken."

"A saucepan, maybe a strainer?"

"No problem."

"A stove?"

She nodded.

"All right, we'll begin by boiling everything. Would you get the saucepan and strainer? I'll ask the other lady to help isolate the Ebola cases. How about the huts?"

"I live in one, you'll be in another. That leaves four for patients."

"Is there a stretcher?"

"We make do with a folding cot."

By sundown, they'd moved the Ebola patients into the unoccupied huts. Only then did Jean-Pierre realize he was exhausted and hungry. "Where can I get a meal? I haven't eaten since this morning on the plane from Paris."

"I do the cooking. Tonight we're having couscous."

He chuckled. "This must be Thursday."

"Yes, it is. Why?"

"Never mind, couscous will be fine."

After serving the patients, they had dinner together in the reception room. When she leaned over him with a plate, he caught a scent he liked, one that reminded him of cocoa butter.

"Tell me about yourself, Ismaïla."

"There's nothing unusual about my life. I was raised and educated in a Catholic orphanage in Bamako. After that, I got a teaching job in Samaflala and married a local politician. I walked out on him when he was arrested for embezzlement. When Ebola broke out in Namba—I was born here, you know—I came back to help."

Working around the clock, it took them the rest of the week to get the hospital operating properly. They wrapped the corpses in plastic and got village women—the men refused to get involved—to overcome their fear and help cremate them. Then they scrubbed down and disinfected the walls, floors, ceilings, and furniture.

The sight of a white man, a stranger, pushing himself to his limits, and his air of confidence and authority, inspired several more women to volunteer. Morale was on the upswing. Particularly his. There was even comic relief from a young English traveler who was having trouble with a tapeworm he'd swallowed on purpose to protect himself from bacteria.

Things were now under control and didn't need Jean-Pierre's constant supervision, so one morning he took the hospital's battered jeep and drove to Samaflala, where he phoned Paris and asked Doctors Without Borders to send qualified nurses.

What Ismaïla lacked in training she made up for in resourcefulness and initiative. She seemed to read his mind and anticipated his every request. A warm friendship evolved.

The strain, however, was taking its toll. One day he noticed she was having trouble concentrating. "Ismaïla, you're pushing yourself too hard. Why don't you take a day or two off and get some rest?"

"No, really, Jean-Pierre, excuse me, I mean Doctor, I'm fine."

He wasn't convinced, but she seemed determined.

The next morning when he entered the hospital's reception room, he found her sitting on a stool, slumped over, hands over her face. When she looked up, it was obvious she was in pain. "Ismaïla, what's the matter?"

"Headache, nausea. I'm sorry."

He put his hand on her forehead. It was hot. Oh my God, he thought, the first symptoms! "Listen, I want you to go to bed immediately." His professional calm was giving way to panic.

"No, Doctor, just get me a couple of aspirins. I'll be all right."

Suddenly she jumped up and grabbed a plastic bag. She had just enough time to clasp it to her mouth before throwing up. Jean-Pierre steered her back to the stool and held her head until she stopped retching. She began to shiver.

He took her by the shoulders and helped her to her feet. "Come on, let's get you to bed."

"No, there's too much to do." She shook him off and turned toward the ward. But before she could reach the door, she collapsed unconscious on the floor. He picked her up, rushed her to her hut, and covered her with a sheet and blanket.

Presently she opened her eyes, looked around, and gave him a wan smile. "All right, I give up." She turned over and fell asleep. He tucked the sheet around her neck and prayed, Please, God, don't let it be!

He remained by her bedside for the rest of the day, watching her closely. The vigil continued throughout the following night, Jean-Pierre occasionally dozing off in his chair. In one restless dream, he was in bed with her, telling her how much he loved her, and she was responding in kind.

When he awoke, it was daylight. Oh my God, he thought, I forgot. The nurses from Paris. They should be landing in Ségou within the hour. Why didn't they take the air taxi to Kambilou? Oh yeah, three of them plus baggage and God knows what else.

He ran toward the hospital to find someone to take over. On the way, he met the village woman who'd just been relieved and was on her way home. He explained about Ismaïla. "Would you watch over her until I get back? Please?"

"Of course, of course! Oh, that's terrible!"

He ran to the jeep and took off. As soon as he was outside the village, he jammed the accelerator to the floor and held it there, careening around corners and throwing up a cloud of dust. Then the road straightened out and his mind wandered. He remembered his dream and wondered if it meant anything.

I wonder what Ismaïla feels for me. I usually can tell but this is a different culture. Maybe the cues aren't the same. Naaa, she probably just likes me.

When the airport came into view, he saw that there was no plane on the ground. Probably late, he thought. He parked and went in the terminal building. An employee wearing an airline jacket and cap looked up. *"Monsieur?"*

"The morning plane from Bamako, when do you expect it?

"It arrived two hours ago."

"Oh no. Were there nurses?"

"I don't know if they were nurses, but there were three young white ladies. They waited around for a while, then paid a man to drive them to Namba."

"Yeah, that was them. Thanks very much."

He ran out, hopped in the jeep and left in a screech of tires. Then he took stock of the situation and muttered, "Come on, no sense risking my ass a second time. They'll know what to do for Ismaïla." He slowed down to a safe speed.

But as he approached Namba, he began to worry again and decided he'd better look in on her right away. He opened the door of the hut quietly so as not to wake her. But she was sitting up in bed, and a nurse in white uniform, her back to him, was listening to her breathing with a stethoscope. When Ismaïla caught sight of him, her face lit up in a wistful smile. "Oh, Jean-Pierre!"

The nurse turned around, and he caught his breath. "Monique, what the hell?"

With a cry of joy, she jumped up and threw her arms around his neck. "Oh, *chéri*, I couldn't help myself. When they told me they needed nurses, I signed up right away. As soon as this is over, I want you to come back to Paris with me. That's where we both belong." She looked into his eyes. "Please don't be angry. I had to come."

Jean-Pierre responded awkwardly to her hug, then backed away.

Ismaïla stared at Monique, then at him.

He held his breath, while Monique, her back turned to Ismaïla, continued to search his face.

Then Ismaïla burst out laughing. Jean-Pierre managed to maintain a semblance of calm.

Ismaïla was obviously feeling much better. "What a wonderful surprise for you, Doctor Fouché. You must be very happy."

Monique looked at Ismaïla, then sadly back at him. "So that's it—you've found a new love."

"Or an old one." He reached for her hand. "Come. Let me take you to our intensive-care ward and I'll show you what one man's first love is: medicine!"

# CREVASSE

"KEEP your voice down, Charlotte. Your Kraut pilot can hear us."

"Come on, Maurice, I interview a lot of Germans on my show. They've changed."

"I still don't see why we had to come to Austria for helicopter skiing. It's just as good in France."

"I wanted you to see that they're no different from us."

"I still don't trust them. Look at him. Blue-eyed, blond, can't you picture him in an SS uniform?"

"You don't understand—this is the *new* Europe. His generation is cursed with the guilt of their fathers. He's doing his best to make this trip enjoyable. Give him a break."

"*You're* the one who doesn't understand. You're not Jewish—your father didn't go through what mine did."

"Maurice, I can't cope with your hate any longer. If you want me to marry you, you're going to have to get over it."

Her tone startled him. This was not the Charlotte he was used to. He searched her face for some sign that she didn't mean it, at least not that strongly. Then he remembered the first

time he'd watched her doing the nightly news. He'd been capti-
vated by her eyes, her smile, her tone of voice; she seemed to be
talking to him alone. But the illusion had been destroyed when
he saw her on twenty screens simultaneously on the shelves of a
TV store. She wasn't just talking to him; she could have had
any man.

Then, miraculously, she'd shown up in his ski class, and
something happened.

"I'm sorry, Charlotte, I'll make an effort."

"Let's go. Klaus wants us to get aboard."

The flight to Teufelshorn Glacier was spectacular, the ter-
rain dramatically rising and falling beneath as they passed over
several crests. The slopes facing the morning sunlight were a
dazzling white, those on the back side a foreboding gray. Between them, majestic crags thrust their callused fists toward the
clear blue sky. In the valleys, they could see villages and pine
forests parted here and there by country roads.

Finally the helicopter soared up a snow-covered slope to its
summit and landed, its downdraft stirring up a thick swirl of
snow. Klaus cut the engine and slid the door open. "All right,
friends, end of the line."

Charlotte got out first. "That was beautiful. Thank you so
much."

Maurice couldn't even nod. His hostility, instilled in him as
a boy by his father's incessant diatribes against the *sales Boches,*
was still too strong.

Klaus attempted to thaw him out. "How did *you* like the
flight?" Maurice merely shrugged his shoulders.

Klaus's smile faded. "I'll get your gear. Carry your things
over there so you won't be under the downdraft when I take off."

While Klaus was opening the tail locker, Charlotte hissed
into Maurice's ear, "At least make an effort to be civil. You
promised, remember?"

He attempted to buy her indulgence with a kiss, but she
turned away, snatched up her skis and poles, and tramped off.

He sighed and followed. When he passed her on her way back to get her backpack, he smiled. No response.

He dropped his skis and poles by hers and went back for his own pack. Still no eye contact. Then he heard a terrified yelp. He turned and saw Charlotte on her stomach clawing at the snow—a crevasse had opened up. Her leg had gone in. As he rushed over to help, Klaus's voice rang out, "Stay back!"

Before the warning registered, his own world turned upside down. He realized he was on his back and Charlotte was clinging to him. His added weight had caused the edge of the opening to give way. They'd fallen twenty feet and landed on an ice bridge covered with snow and extending from one side of the crevasse to the other.

He shuddered at the thought of how they might have died if it hadn't been there to stop their fall. They would have been wedged in between converging walls of ice, slipping in ever tighter each time they let out their breath, broken ribs maybe, and finally suffocating and freezing to death.

Vertical walls of luminescent milky-blue ice rose twenty feet above to an oval opening through which he could see the deep Alpine sky. He started to sit up, but something broke loose and went clattering into the abyss. The sound was crystalline, intermittent, its collisions with the sides sounding off distances as it fell. He pulled Charlotte against him. She was shaking.

Klaus's head appeared above. "Don't move. I have rescue and survival gear in the chopper."

He was back in a few moments. "Damn! They must have taken everything out at the hangar and forgot to put it back. All I have is a rope. We'll have to make do. Listen, I've made a loop. Slip it under your friend's arms. Here it comes."

Maurice's concern for Charlotte momentarily made him forget that Klaus was German. "I understand. Please hurry."

A coil of rope came tumbling toward him. When its slack was taken up, it whipped to a stop eight feet above his head and swung back and forth.

Klaus' voice rang out. "Got it? "

Maurice shook his head. "Not yet."

The rope dropped another two feet. "All right?"

"No, keep coming."

"That's all there is."

"Oh my God," Charlotte wailed.

After a moment of silence, Klaus spoke again. "I'll radio for help. Hang on. Don't move."

Charlotte pressed against Maurice. "Darling," she sobbed, "I'm so sorry. If I hadn't—"

"No, no, you were right. I love you, Charlotte. Don't worry, we'll make it."

Their closeness made them forget the increasing bite of the cold.

A few moments later, Klaus's head reappeared. "They're on their way, but it'll take time. Meanwhile, we have to try to get you out on our own—you mustn't stay in that deep freeze too long."

"What do you suggest?"

"First, sit up, one at a time. But real slow. If the bridge shows no signs of weakness, stand up. Then, Maurice, you lean against the wall and get her up on your shoulders."

Charlotte moaned. "Oh my God, do I have to?"

Maurice gave her a squeeze. "It's all right, he knows what he's doing. You first, you're lighter."

She held her breath and got to her feet. He did the same. The bridge seemed solid enough. He looked up at Klaus. "So far, so good."

"All right, here comes the rope."

"Listen, Klaus, better make the loop just big enough for her hand. That'll give us a little more length. She'll have to stretch as it is." He gave Charlotte an encouraging smile. "Okay, sweetheart, I'm going to cup my hands together. Put one foot in, grab my head, then step up, and get your other foot on my shoulder."

"I'm terrified!"

"Come on, Charlotte, you can do it."

It took her a couple of tries before she succeeded. She had a painful grip on his hair. Her voice was trembling. "All right, now what?"

"Get your other foot up, then stand up."

She moved unsteadily. Maurice reached up and grasped her ankles. "You're doing fine. Now straighten up. Reach up, put your hand through the loop, and grab the rope. The noose will tighten around your wrist."

She was shifting from side to side, and he had to maneuver to stay under her. Suddenly she lost her balance and screamed. But she did manage at the last instant to grasp the rope.

Maurice staggered and fell forward. Now Charlotte's full weight was hanging from the one wrist, and she was crying out in pain. At the same time, she was flailing the air with her legs and struggling to reach the rope with her free hand.

"Stop moving," Klaus yelled, "I can't pull while you're kicking like that." Maurice jumped up and steadied her feet. Then she passed out. Klaus began hauling, and Maurice prayed. When she'd disappeared over the edge, he let out his pent-up breath. "Thank God."

Klaus stuck his head back into view. "She's okay, she's coming to. Listen, I have to move the helicopter closer so I can tie the rope to a strut. Hang on, it'll only take a minute."

The operation took another five minutes, during which the downdraft from the rotors sent snow cascading over Maurice. After some maneuvering, the helicopter settled to the surface and the rotors stopped. The air cleared, and Maurice opened his eyes. He could see the chopper's tail through the opening above. A minute later, the rope dropped back down. He groaned—it was still out of reach. He jumped for it several times, cushioning his landing with bent knees so as not to jar the bridge loose. But a piece broke away, and he didn't dare try again.

Klaus's head appeared again. "How's it going down there? Can you reach the rope?"

"No, and it's getting pretty damned cold."

"Maurice, we're going to change places. I'm coming down. I'll give you a boost like you did with Charlotte. You'll be able to pull yourself up—I've tied knots in the rope."

"But how will *you* get out?"

"Help is on its way. I'll have enough body heat until they arrive."

"I can't ask you to do that."

"*Nein*, I'll be okay."

Klaus let himself down and dropped the last few feet. But when his feet reached the bottom, he slipped and fell on his stomach. Clawing at the surface, he began sliding, feet first, toward the edge.

Without thinking, Maurice grabbed his wrist just as his legs went dangling over. As he did so, the memory of his father's horror stories and the pictures he'd seen of Nazi concentration camps came crashing back—stacks of corpses, ovens, emaciated survivors peering with disbelief from their bunks at their liberators. For a moment, he was tempted to let go. He looked into Klaus's eyes, searching for some trace of evil. There was none—only resignation.

Then he thought, What does Klaus have to do with my father anyway? He didn't ask to be German any more than I asked to be French. Why should his clear blue eyes, light blond hair, and a build like a Greek god automatically make him the enemy? He *did* risk his life to save Charlotte and me. Nobody asked him to. What would I have done in his place? Oh God, forgive me!

Maurice pulled him up.

Klaus turned over, sat up, and took a deep breath. *"Danke, Freund!"* After a long silence, he added, "I'm also glad for *you* that you did that. You would have been torn between hate and guilt for the rest of your life."

Maurice once more became conscious of the biting cold and began flailing his arms around his chest. In a shaking voice, he asked, "Tell me something. Are all Germans as decent as you?"

Klaus grinned. "I was only doing my job." Then his expression became serious. He put a hand on Maurice's shoulder. "But good or bad, don't forget we're all God's children, and that makes us all brothers and sisters."

Maurice realized that everything had now changed. He no longer felt his father's pain and hate, only remorse. "Forgive me, Klaus, I've been blind."

"Come on, let's get you out of here."

"No way. Let's get *you* out."

"*Nein, you* are the client."

"Yes, but—"

Suddenly Klaus looked up at the opening. "Listen."

Maurice strained to hear. At first nothing, but a few seconds later he heard a faint thumping. He looked into Klaus's eyes for confirmation. Klaus nodded, and the sound grew into the triumphant throbbing of a helicopter. They began laughing and yelling. Then, on no apparent cue, they hugged.

Klaus was jabbering in German; Maurice could only understand the emotion of his voice. He grinned. "Yes, brother, we made it."

# THE GOURMET

JEAN-JACQUES, the *maître d'hôtel,* realized at first glance that the corpulent gentleman waiting to be seated was a connoisseur of fine cuisine and vintage wines. With the dignity of an emperor, he was twirling his waxed mustache, leaning on the pommel of his walking stick, and surveying the crowded restaurant. He was barely five feet tall, and his hair was thin, black, neatly parted in the middle, and slicked down on the sides. He wore horn-rimmed glasses and was dressed in a correct navy-blue suit, narrow black tie, and a white shirt that spread over his vast abdomen like a spinnaker in a stiff wind. He nodded gravely as Jean-Jacques approached.

"Good evening, I am Gustave Fournier. I believe you have a table for me?"

"Of course, *monsieur.* Exactly what you requested—a quiet corner. Follow me, please."

To Jean-Jacques, the society of *haute cuisine* had its own hierarchy. Its royalty consisted of the great chefs of the world and a small number of genuine gourmets like Monsieur Fournier. Both lived for those rare moments when they would come together to play their respective roles in the sublime rites of gastronomy. For the chef, preparing and orchestrating a superb meal for someone capable of appreciating its subtleties was the ultimate challenge. For the patron, the pleasures of the palate, nose, and eye were the quintessence of art and sensuality. On such occasions, the *maître d'hôtel* and waiters would watch from a distance, ready like choir boys to step in and perform their assigned roles.

Next was a small number of dedicated *maîtres d'hôtel,* like himself, and wine stewards whose tastes and instincts had been honed to perfection over generations. While never presuming to pass for royalty, they nevertheless considered themselves noblemen of a sort. Then came the *bourgeoisie,* made up of diners with just enough knowledge and taste to claim a small measure of deference. At the very bottom were the poseurs and tourists who came only to see and be seen or to be able to boast later about something they had not the breeding to appreciate. They were tolerated only because their money kept the restaurants solvent.

To Jean-Jacques, nationality was an additional factor; only Frenchmen had the right genetic makeup and cultural background. He held as one of the basic tenets the old adage that while Germans merely feed and Englishmen eat, only Frenchmen dine. As for Americans, he had cried the day McDonald's erected its golden arch on the Champs-Elysées. He had lamented, "From the Arch of Triumph to the Arch of Treason, France is doomed."

He ushered Gustave to an alcove with wall panels of antiqued mirrors and a leather settee. Inside, a small crystal chandelier shed a discreet light on an elegantly appointed table for one with white tablecloth, gold-rimmed bone china, an array of graceful wine glasses, and a panoply of silverware. "Is this satisfactory, *monsieur?*"

"Very satisfactory, thank you."

Jean-Jacques snapped his fingers, and while Gustave eased

himself onto the settee, a waiter in black tie sprang forward to help him slide the table in. Then he presented the menu to him, and the two of them bowed their heads and retreated.

Gustave gestured for Jean-Jacques to come back. "I left a book in the right pocket of my topcoat. Would you mind getting it for me?"

"Not at all, *monsieur.*"

A minute later Gustave had a copy of the *Guide Michelin Gastronomique* open beside the menu and appeared to be making comparisons while taking notes on a pad of paper. The next time the waiter walked by and saw what he was doing, he gasped, hastened to the reception pulpit, and whispered in the *maître d'hôtel's* ear, "The gentleman in the alcove is an inspector for *Guide Michelin.*"

"Oh *mon Dieu!* I'll alert the chef. You take his order. But stay calm."

The waiter wiped the perspiration from his forehead and hurried to Gustave's table. "Are you ready to order, *monsieur?*"

"Perhaps, but there's a slight problem. I have to be at another restaurant in two hours."

The waiter's heart skipped a beat. "Perhaps there is something we can do. I'll be right back."

A few moments later, the waiter returned with the high priest of the kitchen—tall, slim, thin-faced, with an aquiline nose, long sideburns, goatee, dressed in a white smock and high mushroom hat, his two hands clasped over his apron. The waiter introduced him as Jules Savarin.

Gustave looked at the man with interest. "Not a descendant of the great Savarin?"

The chef smiled. "But of course. A direct descendant. What can I do for you? I understand you are in a hurry."

"Yes, that is true. I have less than two hours. What do you suggest?"

"You may be in luck. It happens that one of our regular patrons, the Compte de Valéseaux, who placed his order earlier in the day, just phoned to say that he has been called out of Paris. If his choice appeals to you, it is almost ready."

"May I know what he ordered?"

"Of course. *Foie gras de canard aux agrumes.* Then a *panache de crustacés et sole à l'estragon.* After that, a *Tournedos Rossini.* And for dessert, poached pears in wine."

"Very good, except for the poached pears. I was in Lyon yesterday and had that last evening at Paul Bocuse's restaurant."

"Paul Bocuse! He is one of my good friends. What would you say to a *mousse glacée à l'anis?*"

"Yes, very well. And before dessert I would like a service of Roquefort, then a small salad."

They shook hands and bowed their heads at one another while the *maître d'hôtel,* who was observing from a distance, swelled with satisfaction. This was going to be one of those sublime moments. Here was an inspector worthy of his salt. The chef retreated, and a moment later the wine steward appeared with the wine list. Gustave politely waved it off.

"Thank you. I have already decided. With the *foie gras,* I would like a Corton-Charlemagne. And with the seafood, I presume you have a good year of Puligny-Montrachet?"

The steward was impressed. Unlike most of their patrons, Gustave had pronounced the name as they do in the wine country, that is, without the *t.* "Yes indeed, an eighty-three, by Rolland Thévenin."

"Very good. And with the beef, I think a Romanée-Conti or if you have none, perhaps a Vosne-Romanée."

"I would suggest the first. I still have a few bottles of sixty-seven."

The waiter arrived shortly thereafter with the first course, and Gustave tucked his napkin high on his chest between the buttons of his shirt—one of the signs of a gourmet of the old school. The *foie gras* was impeccable, and Gustave savored every bite, carefully blotting his lips after each sip of wine and coming back to reality from time to time just long enough to jot down a few words on his note pad.

As the third course was served, the wine steward poured out a finger of the Romanée-Conti and watched as Gustave held his glass up to the light, studied the color, twirled the wine, observed the leg of natural glycerin sliding back down the sides, plunged his nose deep inside, breathed in the vapors, and finally took a sip, which he sloshed around in his mouth before swallowing and waiting for the aftertaste. The steward held his breath until Gustave looked up and nodded.

Later, when Jean-Jacques saw Gustave put a piece of Roquefort into his mouth along with a sip of the Romanée-Conti and macerate the mixture before sending it on its way, he knew they were dealing with a Burgundian and prayed they'd done everything right. At one point he looked around and realized he was not the only one who was concerned. The chef was also observing Gustave's every move through the small window set high in the kitchen door.

While Gustave was topping off the meal with a snifter of old armagnac, Jean-Jacques eased himself into the kitchen to confer with Jules. "What do you think? I cannot tell anything from his expression."

"I know. He has not smiled once."

"Perhaps we could assure ourselves of a favorable report if we refused to let him pay."

"No, no! That smacks of bribery." Jules tugged on his goatee for a moment, then lit up. "I have an idea. Tell him that since Paul Bocuse is a mutual friend, I would like him to be my guest this evening."

Jean-Jacques transmitted the message, apologizing that Jules had his hands full and could not come out again. Gustave replied that he was touched but could not accept. Jean-Jacques had to implore him to put away his billfold, which he finally did after a sigh of resignation.

It was a mild evening, and as Gustave went out onto the sidewalk he felt happy and fulfilled. The day had been a success. Nothing more could be done to add to it. He'd dine at the Tour d'Argent the following evening. He decided to walk back to his hotel. But as he passed in front of La Coupole, he was suddenly seized with an irresistible desire for a plate of oysters and a bottle of Crépy. After only a moment's hesitation, he shrugged his shoulders and went in. He had long ago decided that the most reasonable way to deal with temptation is to give in to it without a struggle. Besides, La Coupole was on his list. As soon as he was seated he put his *Guide Michelin* and note pad on the table. Again his money was refused.

He spent most of the next day at a café table on the square Saint-André-des-Arts reading *Le Monde* and watching people pass by. Aside from a croissant and a *café au lait* for breakfast, he ate nothing until evening. When it finally got dark, he strolled down to the quais and followed them east to the Tour d'Argent.

As usual, out came the *Guide Michelin* and the note pad. This time he decided to begin with a *brochet au beurre blanc*, then continue with a *médaillon de boeuf à la crème de champignons*. No point in ordering the house's famous pressed duck— it's excellence was already established beyond question. Then cheese as usual—this time a brie—a salad, and a strawberry tart. As he pondered which wine to have with the beef, the wine steward offered a suggestion.

"May I suggest a Château Ausone?"

"No, no, not a Saint-Emilion. Something softer, rounder, a bit more feminine. Let me see. Perhaps a Médoc. Yes, the Château La Lagune—I see you have some nineteen seventy-seven."

Another perfect repast.

As Gustave was finishing his tart, the *maître d'hôtel* approached. "*Monsieur*, it is not every day that we are honored by a presence such as yours and I would be most pleased if you would accept a glass of cognac."

Gustave was delighted but kept his serious expression. The rules of his occupation allowed him to accept, but disallowed any sign of indebtedness. He nodded, and a few moments later the *maître d'hôtel* was pouring some of the dark colored ambrosia into the bottom of a teacup—a tradition among certain connoisseurs. "Do you mind if I join you?"

"Please! Do sit down, I beg you." Gustave saluted his host with his cup and proceeded to pass it under his nose. His reaction was immediate and instinctive. His eyes opened wide with surprise, and he took a sip to make sure, allowing it to remain for a moment on the surface of his tongue before allowing it to trickle back into his pharynx. "*Mon Dieu*, a Château d'Ambleville!"

The *maître d'hôtel* was equally impressed. "I must say. I've never met anyone with the nose and palate that you possess. The dinner, of course, is on the house. Would you mind very much if I asked a close friend and his companion to have a glass with us? He is also a connoisseur."

Gustave acquiesced, and the *maître d'hôtel* held up his hand and beckoned to a couple, who came over—an athletic-looking man of about thirty and a stylish young lady in her mid-twenties.

"*Monsieur*, I have the honor of introducing Patrick Dufour and Béatrice Barecq." Gustave rose, shook the gentleman's hand, and kissed the lady's. He found her most appetizing but felt that the man looked more like a civil servant than a *bon vivant*. The four of them sat down, and cognac was served to the couple. The *maître d'hôtel* turned to the lady and her escort.

"My friends, since you are interested in *haute cuisine*, I felt you absolutely had to meet *Monsieur*...." He hesitated as if he had forgotten his name. Gustave spoke up.

"Gustave Fournier, at your service."

The *maître d'hôtel* went on. "Monsieur Fournier is an inspector for *Guide Michelin*, isn't that so?"

Gustave nodded.

Patrick Dufour seemed interested. "What a wonderful occupation. I envy you. How long have you been an inspector for Michelin?"

"Oh, for ten years, more or less." But no sooner had the words left his mouth than he felt he'd made a serious blunder.

For a long moment the three just looked at him. Finally Patrick Dufour nodded with satisfaction and produced a police badge while the young woman removed a tiny tape recorder from her handbag and laid it on the table. "Well, I think that's all the evidence we need." A tide of hot blood rushed to Gustave's head, and his heart pounded in his chest. All he could do was blot his lips with his napkin and turn up his palms in a gesture of futility. To his surprise, the three others showed not the slightest sign of triumph.

Patrick rose. "I'm afraid you'll have to cut your cognac short and come with us, Monsieur Fournier."

"But how did you know?"

"A simple stroke of luck, nothing more. A real inspector for *Guide Michelin* went to the restaurant where you dined last evening just after you left. The *maître d'hôtel* remembered your saying you would be coming to the Tour d'Argent, so here we are."

Gustave was given only a short stay in jail. But each single day was intolerable. He felt like a frog out of water—surrounded by ruffians, kept in a depressing cell with almost no amenities, obliged to sleep on a hard bunk, to eat tasteless food and drink vile *vin ordinaire*—life seemed no longer worth living. He stopped eating. Of course he lost weight, his legs became unsteady, his eyes blurred, his mind grew fuzzy.

Then one day a guard appeared at his cell door with a visitor. At first, Gustave just stared. Nothing registered. The man seemed concerned. "Monsieur Fournier, don't you remember? I am Jules Savarin. I cooked for you in my restaurant the day before you were arrested."

Gustave studied the eyes, the aquiline nose and the goatee, and gradually the memory filtered back. The *foie gras,* the *panache de crustacés et sole à l'estragon,* the *Tournedos Rossini* and the extraordinary *mousse glacée à l'anis....* Yes, of course. He nodded in recognition. Savarin sat down on a stool that the guard had brought in.

"I'm so sorry. A man of your taste and breeding. The law is applied by people incapable of appreciating excellence."

The memory of that sublime dinner made tears come to Gustave's eyes too. Jules reached through the bars and took his hands in his. "Please don't. Listen, I know people in high places. Be patient for a moment. I will be right back."

He reappeared, followed by two uniformed waiters carrying a small table the contents of which bulged under a white cloth. The guard opened the cell door and they set it down. Jules whisked the cloth away with a flourish, and Gustave's eyes were greeted by the sight of an elegant service for one. As the metal covers were ceremoniously lifted from the plates, Gustave came to life again. A *bouquet gourmand à la Niçoise, fricasée de cuisses de canard et la daube de champignons des bois,* cheese, a salad and *petits fours.* He shook his head in disbelief.

Jules looked down at him with a compassionate smile. "My friend, I read your dossier. The soul of a sovereign, the purse of a pauper, *n'est-ce pas?*" Then, with a joyful *"Voilà!"* he produced two bottles of wine. "Oh yes, and let us not forget the bread."

Gustave wiped his eyes, picked up the white napkin, tucked it into his open collar, and began to dine in quiet dignity while the two waiters and Jules looked on. When he was finished, he rose, bowed, and said, "Thank you, I am most grateful."

Jules smiled. "Monsieur Fournier, your sentence is not long. I shall send someone every day with something special. When you get out I want you to return to my restaurant as my guest. We must talk about your future."

# THE VOICE

I KNEW I couldn't endure Sarajevo much longer. The French Army had assigned me to the UN Peacekeeping Force, but all I'd done so far was drive an armored vehicle back and forth across an avenue as a shield for people wanting to get to the other side. Why they couldn't stay put was beyond me.

Besides, our mission was hopeless. Even though our blue helmets made our identity unmistakable, we were being shot at and weren't allowed to shoot back. The main accesses for food and medical supplies had been cut off, and all efforts to get the besiegers to back off had failed.

Then one day in January, my unit got orders to escort a team of negotiators out by a back road over the mountains. I knew it would be dangerous. While the area was wooded and would provide cover, it was also a good place for an ambush. At least, I was leaving.

They put together a convoy of small vehicles armed with whatever weapons they could carry. I was assigned to drive a jeep and bring up the rear. My partner, Jacques Leroy, was in the back with a machine gun. The vehicle just ahead was a personnel carrier with a man sitting on top with his back to us, cradling a rocket launcher on his lap.

As we started up the mountain, it began to snow. We pulled our collars up around our necks but were soon wet and shivering. To add to our discomfort, the road was a mess, and we were being bounced around.

As we were grinding up a steep grade, I noticed a wire strung from one tree to another in the haphazard way typical of combat phone lines. I was pondering why the Serbs were using such an antiquated system, when the convoy stopped and the driver of the lead car climbed a tree and cut the line. We finally reached the crest and began picking up speed.

Suddenly the man on the personnel carrier clutched his neck and was catapulted backwards onto the rocky road. A section of the phone line crossing the road had caught him in the throat. His rocket launcher was thrown into the air and landed heavily on his chest. I slammed on the brakes and skidded to a stop inches from his head. We jumped out to help him. He was wheezing and writhing in pain as he struggled to inhale through a crushed pharynx. Then he passed out. He was suffocating. Something had to be done immediately.

I'd had a little first-aid training, so I got out my penknife and lip balm capsule, which I made into a tube by emptying it and prying off the bottom. Then I gritted my teeth, cut an opening through the depression just below his voice box between his collarbones, and pushed the tube through. To my relief, he started breathing normally. By that time, my captain had run up and assessed the situation. "You two take him back to Sarajevo. Where we're going is too far. This man needs help fast."

"Yes sir. Jacques, you drive. I'll take care of him."

We nearly slipped off the road getting turned around but made it and were soon on our way. We had the man stretched out on the back seat, and I was on my knees sponging the blood away from the incision. How much went into his lungs, I couldn't tell. Presently, he came to and tried to speak. When he found he couldn't, he panicked and tried to sit up. I held him down. He nodded and lay back.

But a few minutes later, he shook his head with a look of despair. I took his hand and started talking. "You're going to make it, soldier. Just hang on. We're on our way back to Sarajevo. They'll have you fixed up in no time." That seemed to give him courage. A little color came back into his face. Every once in a while, however, he would writhe with pain and tighten his grip on my hand.

"You're doing fine," I said. "Everything's going to be all right. Come on now, don't give up."

Night was falling. Jacques turned on the headlights without realizing it would make us a perfect target. In less than a minute, a shell exploded in a blinding flash less than fifty meters ahead. He switched them off again, put the jeep into reverse, and we lurched back. As soon as we stopped, a second shell landed right where we'd been. I heard him mumble, "*Merde!* We're gonna have to stay here until morning."

We got the jeep's roof canvas out of the back and put it over our patient. Jacques offered to relieve me, but each time we tried, our casualty would panic and cling desperately to my hand. So I stayed with him and kept talking. "Come on, buddy. Hang on. You're going to make it." Soon my words, the same ones over and over again, began to lose their effectiveness. The look of hopelessness came back to his face. I had to find something meaningful to hold up to him as a reason to live. If he had been able to talk, I could have asked about his loved ones, his home, friends, even his dog if he had one.

He was wearing a wedding band, so I knew he had a wife. What about children? That would depend on his age. I felt in his pockets and found a wallet. I took out my pen light and looked through it, shading the beam with my hand. His name was Luc Leroux, a sergeant, and there was a snapshot of a pretty brunette holding two toddlers in pink on her lap, twins it looked like. Their smile stirred something in me. I gazed at it for a while. He was a lucky man. I had chosen the life of a loner out of fear of losing my freedom, but the price was that I had no one. I turned the picture over. There was handwriting. "Love from your three sweethearts. Cécile." I turned the light on his face. About thirty, handsome. At that age, probably a career soldier.

Now I had something to go on. "Come on, Luc, don't let Cécile and the girls down. They want you back in one piece." That brought a response. He squeezed my hand. So I kept on. "You're doing great, Luc. Hang in there. You have a gorgeous wife and beautiful children. You owe it to them. They love you and want you back. They're counting on us, I mean *you*."

I wondered why I'd said "us." I thought about it and realized that, as their vital link, I had become part of them. If he didn't make it, they wouldn't, and part of me wouldn't either. I looked at the snapshot again and envied him. For the rest of the night, I drew the energy I needed from Cécile and the children.

Nevertheless, I had to fight to stay awake. Whenever my mind became fuzzy and I started to mumble, Luc would squeeze my hand with insistence. But eventually I found myself once more repeating the same things. If I'd had a wife and kids of my own, I could have talked about them, and he might have related to them. I can't remember anymore what I said, but it saw him through. My partner, Jacques, slept all night.

Dawn came with agonizing slowness. Throughout the ordeal, Luc had kept his eyes closed and his lips compressed, trying to shut out the pain. When we pulled up in front of the hospital and I saw the medics approaching, I myself collapsed. I awoke that afternoon on a cot in the hospital and asked about him. A helicopter had taken him to an American aircraft carrier in the Adriatic. He'd be taken care of, they said.

It was eleven months before Jacques and I were sent back to our army base in France. My stint would be over once they'd done the paper work. Meanwhile, there was nothing to do but read, play cards, go to the movies they provided, and stand in line for meals. But for the first time in my life, I was enjoying the company of others. When I wasn't talking with new friends, I'd fantasize about having a wife and children of my own. What I visualized was Cécile and her two girls.

It was during one of those waits in a chow line that someone tapped me on the shoulder. I turned to see, but the face didn't register. The man held out his hand. "I've been looking for you, I mean *listening* for you everywhere."

I gave him a polite shake. "There must be a mistake. I don't know you."

"I don't know you either, but I know your voice."

"My voice?"

"Yes, it's recorded in my brain. It's as if I had a tape recorder in my head. When I heard you talking just now, I knew it was you."

I looked at him. He was dead serious. Then I thought maybe he was crazy. "Look, I honestly don't know what you're talking about."

"You were in Sarajevo last year, right?"

"Yes I was."

"You drove a jeep in a convoy over the mountains, didn't you?" The man wasn't crazy. He went on. "A man was injured."

"You were in that convoy?"

"That was me. I just got out of the hospital a couple of months ago. I've had a real bad time—crushed larynx, internal injuries from landing on a rock and having the rocket launcher come down on me."

"Oh my god. Luc! I'm sure glad to see you. Say, how are Cécile and the girls?"

He looked surprised I should remember his wife's name. "They're fine. They have a room near the base. Cécile has brought me through a very rough time."

I felt like hugging him. "I'm so glad you made it!"

"Yeah, thanks to you."

"Oh, the airway. Sorry I had to cut you open like that."

"It was a lot more than that. I could hear the medics talking while they were prepping me for transportation to the American carrier. They weren't sure I'd survive. I heard one say I was hanging on by a thread. Let me tell you, there's one thing you don't know unless you've been there."

"What's that?"

"When you're that close, death becomes a temptation. It means escape from pain, an end to the struggle." He put a hand on my shoulder. "Would you mind repeating some of what you were telling me in the jeep?"

"Like what?"

"I mean like 'Hang on, soldier. Cécile and the girls are waiting for you. You're going to make it. Everything's going to be all right.'"

I complied, and a look of rapture came over his face.

"Yeah, that's it! How can I ever thank you? All through the ordeal, even when I was out cold during surgery, I kept hearing your voice, like on a tape recorder, encouraging me, telling me not to let go. When I came to, one of the medics said, 'We've got to hand it to you, soldier. You've got a lot of guts.' I remember answering, 'It wasn't me. It was the voice.' Of course they couldn't understand."

Luc shook my hand again, looked intently into my eyes for a moment, nodded, then walked away. Just before he disappeared into the crowd, I called after him "Luc!"

He turned. "Yes?"

"Give my love to Cécile and the kids. And my thanks too, okay?"

"You're thanking *them*? For what?"

I just smiled and waved him off.

# HORIZONS

"THANK you, *Papa*, but I really don't want to go on this trip. The USA is nothing but violence, fast food, and gadgets. The only thing worth seeing is the Grand Canyon."

Charles broke out laughing. "Good lord, Philippe, where did you get that idea?"

"Please, Germaine and I are perfectly happy here in Custines."

"Ah, therein lies the truth."

"What do you mean?"

"All the two of you do is putter in your vegetable garden. You haven't any idea of what's going on in the world."

"*Papa*, since the mill shut down, I've been waiting for a job to open up close to home."

"That's been how long? Two years? Why don't you sell this place and get an apartment in Nancy? There are lots of opportunities and things to do there."

"We don't like big cities."

"Nancy, a big city? You're joking. Tell me, how many times have you been to Paris?"

"Only that once, for Germaine's mother's funeral."

"Did you at least do some sightseeing, go to museums, plays?"

"No, we didn't feel comfortable there. We took the first train home."

"Let me tell you something. If Daum hadn't hired me to promote their crystal ware in America, I'd still be stuck in Nancy, and my horizons would be as limited as yours. You've got to start putting things into perspective."

Just then, Germaine emerged from the kitchen bearing an antique Quimper serving dish with a steaming eight-egg omelet garnished with truffles and herbs. She set it down on the checkered tablecloth in front of her father-in-law while Philippe uncorked the wine.

Charles filled his lungs with the aroma. "Germaine, you are as much a culinary artist as you are lovely and charming. But it seems to me you go to a lot of trouble doing everything the way your grandmother did—wire eggbeater and all that. What do you have against modern appliances?"

"They take all the art out of cooking."

Philippe poured a finger of wine into his glass, twirled it, held it up to the light, sniffed it, took a sip, agitated it with his tongue, then with a nod, poured, first for his father, then for Germaine and himself.

For a few minutes, nothing more was said, the three of them relishing Germaine's superb breakfast. While Charles was concentrating on the food, Philippe shot a raised-eyebrow look at his wife and turned both palms upward. She pressed her lips together and slowly shook her head, thinking, Papa Charles has been so good to us, I hope Philippe isn't going to spoil everything.

Philippe gave in with a sigh. "How long will we be gone?"

"Actually this will have to be a quick trip. I'll need two days in Los Angeles and two in San Francisco. That'll leave us two weeks. I'm scheduled to go to Japan afterward."

Germaine shook her head. "Two weeks? That's enough time to see any country from end to end and top to bottom."

Charles laughed and blotted his mouth with his napkin. "Pass the baguette, please. Say, what kind of wine is this?"

"It's a *Côtes de Toul*, local, almost."

"Not bad at all."


A week later, Charles and Philippe were driving through central Nevada on a secondary road Charles had chosen to show his son how the "Wild West" used to look. They hadn't seen a sign of life for the past hour, except for two vehicles passing in the opposite direction. The desert extended to the horizon in all directions, at times rolling or flat, at times broken into illogical ridges and gullies, with bone-dry mountains and desert scrub surviving in a precarious margin between life and death. The drive to Las Vegas had already unsettled Philippe, and when they stepped out of their air-conditioned car into the hundred-and-fifteen-degree heat to relieve themselves, he gasped. "A person could die out here!"

"But it's pure grandeur, isn't it, Philippe?"

"Yes, perhaps, but in a hellish way. These distances are simply not on a human scale. There's too much to comprehend."

Another half hour went by before he said another word. "Look, *Papa*, there's something up ahead." For the moment, it was only a speck by the side of the highway, but five minutes later they saw it was an ancient weather-beaten gas station. An old man on a chair tilted back against the wall of the shaded drive-in area, his feet propped up on an up-ended nail cask, looked up from his reading and waved as they sped by.

Philippe shook his head. "You'd have to be crazy to want to live out here."

They hadn't gone another mile when there was suddenly a bang and the car went into a flip-flopping sway. Charles tightened his grip on the wheel and let up on the gas. "*Merde*, our left rear tire." They slowed and pulled onto the shoulder.

Charles went around back, looked at the wheel, and opened the trunk. "Look, no spare. Oh well, there's enough rubber left to take us back to the gas station."

When they pulled into the station, the man got up and ambled over and looked at the damage. "Lucky it happened here. Nothing for the next forty miles."

"I don't suppose you have tires."

"No, nearest tire store is in Ely. But I think I can help. Hang on a minute." He disappeared inside and emerged a minute later with a grin. "Son of a rancher a couple of miles over there said he'll take you to Ely and back. Coming right over. Let's take that wheel off and remove what's left of the tire."

Presently a cloud of dust appeared in the direction the man had pointed to, and the black dot stirring it up grew into a figure on a motorcycle. The sound didn't reach them for another minute. It was only a hum at first, but it amplified into a growl and finally a roar as the boy—in checkered shirt, jeans, and turned-around baseball cap—came to a dusty skid-turn on the gravel. He waved a greeting at the old man, got off, said "Howdy" to Charles and his son, and secured the wheel onto his luggage rack. "Okay, sir, climb on." Charles straddled the seat behind the boy, and they sped away.

The man turned to Philippe. "Name's Luke. Come on in and have a beer, it's getting hot. You're French, aren't you?"

Philippe nodded and followed. Luke led him through the gas station and up a flight of stairs to a rustic apartment. "Just a second, I'll get the beers."

While he was in the kitchen, Philippe looked around. One wall was covered by bookshelves with dozens of paperbacks and hardcovers. A sophisticated-looking stereo system occupied the opposite side. A cello stood in one corner. There was more to the man than he'd suspected. He went over to the bookshelves. *Tiens*, Shakespeare, Henry James, even Proust in English. What about his music? Let's see, Mozart, Beethoven....

Luke was back with a bottle and two glasses. "Okay, come on out and enjoy the view. How's your English?"

"Not very good, but I can understand if you do not speak too rapidly."

Luke led Philippe through a rear door and onto a spacious veranda covered by an awning. An arid valley fell away at a steep angle for a few hundred feet then flattened out and extended for miles to a mountain range on the horizon. The vastness and silence stirred up emotions Philippe had never felt—something like being in a cathedral. He drew in his breath.

Several rustic armchairs with low tables at their sides faced the panorama. Luke motioned toward them, and they sat down.

While Luke filled the glasses, Philippe studied his profile. There was a subtle dignity and elegance about him that he hadn't noticed before the books and CDs made him take a closer look. But why live way out here, apparently alone? "Pardon me, I don't mean to be indiscreet, but you do not mind this isolation?"

Luke looked out over the valley and shook his head. "I love it out here—the quiet, the purity, the grandeur. I spent fifty years in the insurance business in San Francisco. My wife died the year before I retired. By that time, I'd had enough of the city and the hassle that goes with it. So I bought this place."

"Why a gas station?"

"It came with the view. I keep it going partly for the ranchers—they're good company—and partly because it gives me a change from my other activities."

"I don't know if I could get used to the emptiness of your West and the distances between places. Maybe it's because I come from a small country."

Luke laughed. "No, even Americans who've spent their lives in populated areas react like you. You see, to me this valley is not a huge expanse of nothingness between what you call places. This *is* a place, a real place between little points on the map that do nothing but clutter up the world."

Philippe thought, Custines is a place, a very little place to be sure, but I don't think it clutters. It's comfortable, good. But I'll admit it doesn't open onto limitless horizons like this. Maybe this fellow has hit on something important out here.

"When you live in one of those little desert towns," Luke continued, "your mind shrinks, because all you're interested in is what's there under your nose. Out here, you expand. You become less attached to little things. During the day, you can look at the mountains way out there and let your imagination range from one end to the other. In the evening, we have our sunsets, the most spectacular in the world. And at night, you can gaze up through a clear sky at more stars than city folks ever see."

Philippe let his eyes wander over the panorama and began to see. There was indeed beauty here, there was grandeur, there was truth. God might very well be present. Still he felt insecure—there was too much.

His father returned, and the boy helped him get the wheel back on. Charles held out a twenty-dollar bill. "Thanks, mister, but I can't take that. I had to run an errand in Ely anyway. Glad to help out."

"Please, I insist."

The boy saw he meant it. "Well, why don't you just pay for the gas. That's all I'll take, really."

Charles gave in and shook his hand. Once Luke had filled the tank, the boy sped away with a wave and a grin. Charles pulled out the twenty-dollar bill again, added another, and handed them to Luke. "This is to fill his tank as long as this holds out."

Two days later, they crossed the Sierras at Tioga Pass and took the road into Yosemite Valley. When they rounded the last curve, the sight of the soaring granite faces of El Capitan and Half Dome rising from the forested floor made Philippe's mouth drop open. Charles noticed but refrained from intruding. He could tell his son hadn't yet reached the turning point. The next few hours might well do the trick.

Presently, they were trudging up the trail toward Nevada Falls. When they got to the top, Philippe was puffing. "*Papa*, you're pretty tough for a man nearly sixty."

"I stay in shape so I can do things like this. Come over here and look out over the falls. What do you think?"

"Spectacular. You know, I think I might actually get to like this country."

"You haven't seen anything yet. If you're game, I want to take you to one of my favorite spots."

Philippe nodded, and Charles led him up a trail through the forest to the foot of the smooth round back of Half Dome, rising imperiously against a deep blue sky. Philippe looked up. "That looks awfully steep."

"Come on. If I can, you can. I'll be right behind you. There's no danger. Just hang on to the cables."

Parallel cables attached to metal bars set upright in the rock and lengths of two-by-four laid crossways provided hand and footholds.

It was over twice as steep as a staircase, and the view below, dwarfed by the height, made Philippe grit his teeth. But he couldn't permit himself the humiliation of begging off.

The cables ended where the dome began to round off. He advanced on all fours toward the edge of the vertical front face. When it got flat enough, he stood up. Charles hung back.

A bald eagle was strutting along the edge and stopping every few feet, its talons spread out on the granite, to look down with fierce intensity into the canyon over two thousand feet below. Philippe held his breath; he'd never seen such a gigantic bird. When it caught sight of him, it turned and looked straight into his eyes. There was something eerily human in the gesture, and it struck Philippe as a challenge.

Then the bird extended its wings, and with a powerful

spring, soared out over the abyss. A few hundred feet out, it banked in a wide arc, circled around to the back of the dome, then swooped down over the top, letting out a loud scream directly over Philippe's head.

Philippe held his breath. *Mon Dieu*, that's magnificent. I wonder what an eagle feels. It must be marvelous—that mastery over everything it sees, that freedom.

He watched, fascinated, as the eagle caught an updraft and soared away, its huge wings practically immobile as if embracing the world below. Philippe watched it grow smaller in the distance and finally disappear. A sadness invaded him. A bond had been formed, and he felt he should be flying alongside the eagle instead of remaining earthbound. He sighed and turned his attention once more to the panorama before him.

Suddenly he felt happy. Something about the incident had liberated him. Beyond the sharply delineated mountains across the canyon, he could make out several other crests, and in the distance, a hazy suggestion of the central valley. Luke's words back in Nevada echoed in his memory—*Out here, you expand.*

He remained motionless for a long time. Then he thought about Custines and Germaine and smiled. They started back down in silence. He knew his father understood.

# A SHADE OF DIFFERENCE

THE moment I stepped out of the Airbus into the tropical night of Senegal, I felt uneasy. I was no longer in the protective cocoon of French white society, and my only thought was to get my job done and return to Paris.

The French Government was helping this country's economy by promoting the consumption of peanuts at home. My assignment was to inspect the plantations, assess the yield of the crops, and arrange for the construction of a peanut-butter processing plant.

I followed the other passengers across the tarmac through a gauntlet of black policemen. The chaos inside the terminal was even more disquieting. When I presented my passport to the immigration officer, my hands were sweating. He slammed his stamp down on it and with a scowl waved me on. "Welcome to Senegal."

I let the air out of my lungs and went to pick up my bag and meet the pilot who was to fly me to Empada. I spotted my name on a piece of cardboard above the heads of the crowd. I pushed through and was greeted by an athletic-looking young black man about my age in dark pants and a white shirt.

"Monsieur Dufourq? I'm Mabana Boi. I'm your air-taxi pilot. Sorry your plane was delayed. It's too dark to fly to Empada now—no lights, you know. I got you a room in Dakar."

A kid in rags tugged at my sleeve and pointed at my bag. I nodded, and Mabana led us out to the sidewalk. A shouting mob of beggars, peddlers, and urchins surged in. I recoiled as a toothless derelict with no legs, seated on a home-made skateboard, propelled himself toward me by paddling against the cement with bare knuckles. When I reached out to pay my little porter, the other children clawed at my hand. Mabana yelled at them to get back, took the money, and gave it to the boy, who ran off with the others in pursuit.

Later, unable to fall asleep, I was bothered by the way I'd reacted at the airport. I finally rationalized that it was the insecurity of being in a Third-World country for the first time. I'd never thought I was a racist, and yet I couldn't deny the condescending attitude I'd always had toward non-whites.

I turned the light back on and picked up a book left on the bedside table—*Ambiguous Adventure,* by Cheikh Hamidou Kane, a Senegalese author. Perhaps it would put me to sleep. That was all I expected, but it turned out to be a work of literary quality, and I couldn't put it down.

The next morning we flew to Empada. A bush taxi took me to Kombano, my final destination. My host was a cheerful young man of about twenty-five named Mamsanou. He greeted me with a handshake and led me to my quarters—a bungalow reserved for VIPs. The furnishings, I later realized, were deluxe compared to how most Senegalese live. The bed was a one-by-two-meter cement platform with a straw tick and clean bedding. Beside that, I had only a table and a chair.

Mamsanou took me to an open-sided pavilion for dinner. As we went in, my attention was drawn to a young native woman in a colorful *boubou* and turban supervising the cooking. She had the face of a goddess—delicate features, black skin with a purplish hue, high cheekbones, sensuous lips, and spar-kling eyes whose changing expressions seemed to cast light and shadows around her like the play of clouds and sun on the countryside.

Mamsanou called her over. "Monsieur Dufourq, this is my sister Ladi."

After kissing him on both cheeks, she gave me a terse hand-shake and returned to her work.

During dinner I couldn't help staring. Afterwards, I told Mamsanou I found her interesting and would like to talk to her.

He shook his head. "That might be difficult to arrange. Be-ing seen talking with a white man might be misinterpreted. She's had problems."

He saw I was disappointed. "Well, maybe she can tag along as I show you around; I'll ask her."

He got her to agree, and she accompanied us on several walks. As long as we were within sight of village people, she re-mained quiet and reserved. When we were alone, however, an-other personality emerged. She was intelligent, educated, and sure of herself. She'd studied in Paris, was divorced, and was now teaching at the regional grade school.

I wanted to draw her out. "Tell me about your experiences in Paris. It's my home town, you know."

"Frankly, I found your city cold, impersonal, and much too big. If I hadn't been lonely and homesick, I wouldn't have got-ten into the mess I did."

"Oh?"

She hesitated a moment. "A fellow student—a white boy—befriended me, and I fell in love. Then one day I overheard him bragging to his friends. All he wanted was to seduce women of as many races as he could. He already had his eye on his next prey—an Arab girl.

"So I came home and married a Senegalese. Mistake num-ber two. After I had my baby, he took a second wife. That's le-gal in our country.

"I couldn't understand it—a stupid sixteen-year-old who did nothing all day but listen to the radio. Then he had the gall to order me and my baby out of the bed onto a mat on the floor. Rather than submit to that indignity, I left him.

"Word of my affair in Paris and my divorce eventually reached Kombano and turned people against me. When Moussa—he's my son—reaches manhood, I'll probably move to Dakar. They're more open-minded there."

Over the next two weeks, we saw a lot of each other. It was clear she felt comfortable in the company of someone who was not a local. Our conversations were mostly about Paris, which she obviously missed, and life in Senegal. I had no doubts about it—we were fast becoming friends.

However, her dazzling beauty, charm, unassuming elegance, and intelligence gradually overpowered me. My feelings grew into desire. One day in a burst of emotion, I took her hand.

She withdrew it. "Please, Patrice, I can't."

When her school year began, our walks were discontinued. I asked Mamsanou to do what he could so I could see her again. I gathered it took some coaxing. She finally gave in, and the three of us had dinner together one evening. Mamsanou had to leave early, so I walked her home.

I was falling in love and couldn't conceal it any longer. When we stopped in front of her hut, I tried to take her in my arms. She pushed me away. "I wish you hadn't done that."

"Ladi, I can't stop thinking about you. I need you. I want you."

"Listen, this has already gone too far. I mustn't see you anymore."

I returned to my hut and lay down, saddened and humiliated. An hour later, there was a knock. I opened the door. "Ladi!"

She looked grim. "At least I can offer you tea."

As she slid past, her breast grazed my arm. My adrenaline

surged. She set the tray down and looked around. "Not exactly a Paris apartment, is it?" Our eyes met, and she came into my arms. I was overwhelmed. "Oh, Ladi, I adore you!"

We made love, though I felt she didn't have her heart in it.

She began coming regularly to my bungalow. She also gave up trying to dissuade me from telling her how much I loved her. But whenever I asked her how she felt about me, she'd merely look into my eyes as if trying to read my mind. I offered to give up my friends in France, my job, even settle in Senegal if she'd marry me.

That finally got a response. "You'd do all that?"

"Anything. I can't live without you."

She chuckled. "If I did agree to marry you, you'd have to convert to Islam."

I took that as a hopeful sign and thought, Why not? I don't take my religion seriously anyway; being Moslem wouldn't make any difference. I nodded.

Then she grinned. "You know, of course, all our men are circumcised."

I winced. "Oh?"

"This isn't Europe, Patrice. We can't take or leave our traditions as we like. Besides, it's a great honor." Then she had an idea. "Listen, there's going to be a *tégu* at the end of the week. Why don't you come and see?"

"A *tégu*, what's that?"

"Our circumcision ceremony. My son is among the boys who will be passing into manhood."

I said I'd go.

The night before the event, the countryside throbbed with drums, and the next morning there was excitement in the air. Mamsanou drove the three of us in an ancient Land Rover. A few kilometers down the road, we turned off into the bush, passing dozens of tribesmen, women, and children. The men were dressed in purple skirts, red Islamic fezzes, and T-shirts with everything printed on them from "Coors Light" to "UCLA." The women wore long *boubous* and turbans. Most had plastic sandals.

Our destination was a clearing around a huge kapok tree. Three drummers were setting up by the trunk. Mamsanou stopped the car. "Let's sit on the hood; we'll see everything from there."

There were already over two hundred Senegalese; I was the only white person. Eventually the drums started a driving beat. The warriors formed a circle two to four thick around the edge of the clearing and began shuffling counterclockwise in rhythm. Mamsanou explained. "Half the circle represents one tribe, the other half their enemy." I watched as one side brandished spears, rifles, umbrellas and other symbolic weapons, while the other sang defiantly in unison. After a while, they exchanged roles. This went on for nearly three hours without any apparent repetition—a ceremony thousands of years old driven by the energy of tradition.

I nudged Mamsanou. "What are they singing?"

"Taunts and threats."

"Who's directing?

"Over there. Two drums do the rhythm. The third one talks. It tells them what to do. Now, if you'll excuse me, there are some people I have to say hello to. I'll be back."

Besides the drums, participants were shaking cans of seashells, blowing zebu horns and referee's whistles, and there was much laughing and shouting. A blast from an ancient muzzleloading rifle made me jump. I turned to Ladi. "Good lord, what's that?"

"It's to scare off evil spirits."

"When do the boys get circumcised?"

"Afterward. They'll stay secluded in the forest for four days. When they come out, they'll be men. I just hope Moussa won't suffer too much."

"What kind of anesthetic do they use?"

"The imam rubs a plant on their penis, that's all."

I had visions of the imam cutting off my foreskin with a rusty razor, scissors, an old penknife, whatever, and I crossed my legs.

Ladi laughed and put her hand on my thigh. "Having second thoughts?"

"No, but can't I have it done in a hospital, by a doctor, with a real anesthetic?"

"You'd actually go through that for me?" For the first time, she seemed to be taking me seriously.

"Of course, anything. Does that mean you'll marry me?"

Her expression saddened. "You're a good man, Patrice."

The rhythm changed to a samba. In the center, an old man began prancing around his spear, holding it vertically, its point to the ground. Several women gathered around, urging him on with intricate flamenco-style clapping.

Ladi explained. "He's reenacting heroic exploits."

Several other similar groups followed. As the exaltation mounted, the participants seemed to lose their identities and metamorphose into one pulsating organism. My own heartbeat quickened.

The next day the imam called on me. "Monsieur Dufourq, Ladi has gone too far. She shouldn't have accompanied you to the *tégu*. She is no longer welcome in Kombano. Why don't you announce you intend to be married in Dakar? What you actually do after you've gone is your own business."

My work was now finished, and Ladi arranged to leave with me on the bus. Her son was now a man and could take care of himself. He'd be staying with his uncle.

Once we were on our way, I asked, "Well what's your answer?"

She hesitated before answering. "There's something I want you to see first in Dakar. I'll tell you then. Meanwhile, no more questions, all right?"

The morning after our arrival, she led me to the port, and

along with a crowd of tourists, we boarded a motor launch. I could see an island about a mile and a half off shore.

"Is that our destination?"

"Yes, it's called Gorée Island."

On the way over, we leaned our elbows on the rail. Ladi seemed sadder than ever. "Patrice, there's something I have to tell you. You know about the earlier men in my life and what they did to me. I was still very bitter when I met you, and when you began making advances, I thought all you wanted was an easy conquest. That's when I decided I could play the game too and get even. I'd make you fall in love with me, then make you suffer. Only I discovered you were not like I thought, and I became involved in a way I hadn't intended."

She turned and looked into my eyes. "I'm so sorry I misjudged you. Please forgive me."

"There's nothing to forgive. That's all behind us." I kissed her, and no more was said until we disembarked. I was filled with happiness.

Ladi, however, was strangely silent. As soon as we landed she took my hand, led me down the jetty, around the beach, and toward a foreboding building where sightseers were gathering. A sign above the door read MAISON DES ESCLAVES.

A guide led us inside. "Ladies and gentlemen, welcome to Gorée Island, one of Africa's ports for the exportation of slaves. That infamous trade was begun in the fifteenth century by the Portuguese, principally to supply labor for the Spanish sugarcane plantations after the expulsion of the Arabs. Later, up to thirty million slaves, bought from African chiefs and traders in exchange for fabrics, spirits, guns, and so forth, were sent to the Americas.

"Before concluding the sale, the buyers examined each captive's muscles, the line of their legs, length of their arms, the condition of their teeth, and made them run, jump, and move all their joints to make sure they were in good condition. Those they took were collared and attached to a chain and put to work.

"Just before they were shipped out, they were branded on the shoulder with the company's initials. There were, of course, revolts, and the reprisals were harsh. People were shot and even stretched out on pieces of wood and quartered. Escape was almost impossible, as the sharks around the island were fed to keep them around.

"But all that was only the beginning of the suffering. Many died on the boats, and the cruelty and humiliation they endured in captivity is well known.

"And it has never stopped. Since Gorée, there have been Auschwitz, Bosnia, Burundi, Zaïre, and the list goes on. It doesn't look as if we'll ever learn, does it?"

He stopped, and no one said a word. The sight of the dank prison, its holding rooms, the narrow door leading out to the embarkation quay, the display of shackles, guns, and other instruments of torture brought everything he'd described to life. A woman behind us began to sob. Several others moaned. Otherwise, silence, broken only by the intermittent breaking of waves outside.

Still holding my hand, Ladi led me away and up to an ancient fort with its rusting World War II big-gun battery. We sat down on a parapet overlooking the cove and jetty. It was a long time before she spoke again. "Patrice, if you truly love me, promise me one thing."

"Of course, anything. What?"

"No, promise me first."

"All right, I promise."

"I want you to remain seated right here for an hour, no matter what."

I was bewildered, but I agreed.

She leaned over and gave me a lingering kiss. "Patrice, my love, I brought you to Gorée so you'd understand that I'd be betraying my people if I said yes." She put a finger over my lips to keep me from saying anything. "You promised." Then she stood up and walked away.

Some time later I was brought out of my stupor by a horn blast in the cove. I looked down. The launch was pulling away.

# ON THE ONE PAW

I'M a female French Poodle, and they call me Fifi. *Tudieu*, how I loathe that name. And the way I'm groomed. Humiliating. They've tried every style there is on me—Shawl, Kennel, English Saddle, Royal Dutch, Puppy, you name it. Right now I look like a set of bottle brushes.

They say my breed is the most intelligent of canines. Actually, humans haven't a clue. They think *they've* domesticated *us*. The truth is, we've conned *them* into providing us with creature comforts.

I'll admit our condition has its drawbacks, but it's a lot better than the so-called wild kingdom. It's really dangerous out there, you know, all the violence, never knowing when and where you'll get your next meal or become someone else's. But it's a pretty fair exchange. We guard their houses, play with their children, sympathize with them, guide them if they're blind.

But a dog's lot isn't the same from one country to the next. In some ways, we're better off in America than in France. The trouble with the French is that they never agree on anything.

Except sex, which I suspect most of them do to compensate for their distrust of one another. It's a lot simpler with us. No hang-ups, just good clean fun. "That was great, buddy. See you around." What's wrong with that?

Unfortunately, we French dogs have picked up some of our masters' bad attitudes. One of these is that we all hate each other, while dogs in the United States have created a laid-back society, based on, believe it or not, the French motto, which incidentally the French never observe, namely, "Liberty, equality, and fraternity." They even have a barking code here for news, gossip, and socializing. It gives American dogs a feeling of togetherness I never felt in France.

But to get on with my story, only don't expect much dialogue—dialogue is a human language thing—my own troubles began when my French master and mistress split up because of their pig-headedness and sold me to a pet store. Well, I hadn't spent half a day there when I was bought by a circus animal trainer named Sparky. As a loving pet? You're kidding, *n'est-ce-pas?* You're forgetting, that was back in France. You want to know how much the French love their dogs? They all swear they do, but when they go on vacation, many of us get dumped by the side of the road, in rest-stop parking lots, almost anywhere.

Pardon me, I have to scratch. Damned fleas. Butch must have given them to me. Small price, though. He was fun. *A propos*, our spiritual leader—an Eastern European Mastiff now living in Italy—insists that abstinence is the only way to stop the spread of fleas. I don't know whether he was neutered at birth and never had sex, or if he's just too old to remember. Come on, Pappy, lighten up. This is almost the twenty-first century.

Okay, where was I? That's right, the circus. Sparky needed me for an act with an elephant. You know, the elephant runs around the ring, and the dog races around beside him, springs up on his back, stands up on his hind paws, then on his front paws, does somersaults and other stupid stunts. I knew what he wanted—I'd seen the act on TV—but I had to play dumb for a while in order not to blow my canine cover.

Did I like it? Yuk! You can't imagine the smells, the filth, that repulsive dry dog food, getting transported from one place to another in a cage, all that and no tenderness or companionship. The elephant in question—his name was Goliath—was a loathsome, unkempt, stupid beast, who thought he was the king of the circus.

You know what makes elephants stupid? Simple. They like to show off that they can recognize sixty words, more or less. What does that get them? Slavery. All the words they learn are commands. "Tote that barge, lift that bale, you've a dumb-looking trunk and a stupid little tail."

Actually, the only other species I respect is cats. They're smart and proud, and they keep themselves clean. On the other paw, they're not open and frank like us. They're selfish little schemers who've conned their masters into pampering them to an outrageous degree. Maybe I am, like you say, jealous of their cushy life, but I can't help it. I just don't like cats.

Okay, back to my story. The Winter Circus toured all of western Europe until April. The country I enjoyed most was Germany. The male German Shepherds would go ape when I was taken for walks. Female French dogs turn them on. I'll admit it was flattering. They'd strut around me and pretend to lead the way. I knew they would have liked to sniff more closely, but my trainer carried a cane and kept them at a distance. Too bad in a way—they're a strong and handsome bunch. A bit too competitive for my tastes, though. I noticed that when they mark a wall or a tree trunk, they twist their torso around so as to squirt as high as possible to make others think they're twice as big as they really are. The only danger in that country was the jealous females. I would have explained I wasn't trying to seduce their males, but I don't know how to bark in German and never could figure out their stiff Teutonic body language.

Around the first of May, the circus would leave by boat for its annual summer tour of Canada and the United States. That's when the accident happened. We were performing in Stamford, Connecticut, when I slipped on manure and clumsy Goliath stepped on my paw. My trainer scooped me up, carried me out, and yelled for the vet. He was upset, and for a second I thought he cared. Well, he was concerned all right. Not for me but only for his stupid act.

The vet came in and wiggled my paw. That hurt so bad I howled. After another minute of torture, he shook his head and said, "She sure as hell can't perform anymore. What shall I do with her?"

"Put her to sleep. She's no use to me that way."

I couldn't believe it. I looked at him and wagged my tail to get him to reconsider. Nothing, not even a glimmer of sympathy.

Just then, an elegant young lady, maybe thirty—that's young for humans—burst in. "Oh, that poor doggy!"

For a second I forgot my injury—she had a French accent.

Sparky turned on her. "What are you doing here? This is a restricted area."

This lady, however, was not one to be bullied. She looked him in the eye and said, "Step aside, please. How bad is it?"

"She's finished."

I was desperate. Then it occurred to me that she might be my salvation. I put on a wistful expression and wagged my tail, this time more energetically. She stroked my head for a second, thinking, then lit up. "May I have her?"

Sparky shrugged his shoulders. "Sure. Why not?"

There *was* a God. I looked up at the sky and thought, Thank you, Canis Maximus.


The lady's name was Babette Mills. She was a Parisian married to an American. They lived in an upper-crust neighborhood called Hilton Park in nearby Darien. No kids. I was it. As soon as we got there, Babette had a top veterinarian look at my paw, which turned out not to be broken, and I was laid up for only a week. The situation looked promising. She was kind, and almost every house on the street had a dog or two.

The problem was that she was obsessed with elegance and status, which nearly led to a disaster the first time she let me out to explore. She dressed me up in a red wool doggy jacket—she must have thought my clipped body needed it despite the fact it was summer—then sprayed me with her perfume, Chanel's "Allure." Don't forget, when it comes to scents, I'm infallible.

Anyway, I started out, head high, anxious to make a good impression. But the reception I got was not what I'd hoped for. With my pompon grooming, the jacket, and oh yes, I forgot the ribbon in my hair, plus the fact that my natural scent was masked by Babette's perfume, the other dogs mistook me for an alien, and I suddenly found myself surrounded with angry snarls, curled-back lips, and bared fangs. In a panic, I flipped over on my back, curled my tail between my legs as far as it would go, and played submissive. But that didn't convince them. I had to pee all over myself like a scared puppy before they stopped. Then a gorgeous Dalmatian stepped in for a sniff.

I could see he was the leader of the community. Satisfied that I was a dog, he wagged his tail, and joyous barking broke out all around. Then he bounded off. Another nudged me, and I understood we were to follow. He led us down the street, across a lawn, around the back of a stately home and dove into the swimming pool. I skidded to a halt at the edge but was immediately butted in from behind—the Dalmatian had decided I needed a bath. I didn't relish the dunking, but I knew I was accepted.

The first months in Darien were very happy. The neighborhood dogs did everything they could to make me feel welcome. It was only after that first period of wild, heedless romps, when I had gained enough confidence to assert myself, that things began to deteriorate.

American dogs are indeed laid back, but at the same time, like their masters, they're conformists, and peer pressures in this country are strong. Being French, I was unfamiliar with American politically correct behavior and etiquette, so as I began being my true self again, I made blunders.

First was the animal rights movement. It had started when they heard about Asia. People actually *eat* us there. Can you believe that? *Quelle horreur!* Anyway, my new canine community decided it wasn't politically correct to slaughter animals for food. However, their boycott only included horsemeat. Like humans, their altruism only went so far as not to deprive them of anything they liked, for example, beef, chicken, and lamb. As for me, I like horsemeat—it's a French thing. Well, the first time they smelled it on my breath, I knew something was wrong.

Then, there was the racial issue. They'd decided it wasn't PC to chase cats or birds anymore. So when they saw me take off after a flock of bluejays, I lost another point.

They probably considered me a snob, which I absolutely am not. I'd been bred to trot along proudly with my head held high, while they usually kept their noses to the ground and sniffed their way along. Also, they'd stop at every tree and fire hydrant, sniff to see who'd been there, then add their own signature. Well, I didn't consider it ladylike. Also, there was the evening bark. After everyone had been confined to his own back yard, they'd start a ruckus but this time for no other reason than to make noise. I found this puppyish and didn't join in.

More serious was the fact that, unlike everyone else, I wouldn't kowtow to Reginald, the big drooling English Bulldog, who would have been the leader of the neighborhood if he hadn't considered it beneath his dignity. Whereas every other nationality merely *thinks* it is the best, English canines are absolutely convinced of their superiority, and American dogs, with their complexes, feel they have to play their game. Reginald's hallmark was his accent, which gave him the privilege of barking the evening news. He didn't sniff trees or fire hydrants either.

Reginald was the only one in the neighborhood who remained aloof to me. But one day, when I stopped to smell a rose, I suddenly felt something wet and cold—you know where. I wheeled around and found myself facing him. He must have been particularly hard-up that day, as he looked down on Frenchies. I bared my teeth and growled at him to leave me alone. You should have seen the surprise on his face, as if I should have been flattered.

What finally made me a total outcast was the male poodle from the housing development on the other side of Arbor Avenue. The dogs from my neighborhood, despite their disclaimers, were fiercely territorial about Hilton Park. They never ventured beyond its limits, and whenever a dog from outside wandered over, he was chased away.

I like to explore, so one afternoon, I set out to see the rest of town. As soon as I crossed the line, a group of happy canines ran up to greet me. After the initial introductions, they led me on a trotting tour. The way their tails were wagging, I could tell they were up to something.

The miracle happened when we turned down Colony Street. The leader of the pack barked, and a handsome male poodle, slightly larger than me, came out from behind a house at the other end.

*L'amour* at first sight, what I'd been dreaming about all my life. The others hung back, watching, as we trotted toward each other. When we were just a few jumps apart, I stopped and waited. He approached rapidly, stiff and formal, coming to a stop when we were slightly past one another, each with our head alongside the other's neck. I sneaked a quick glance, then looked away. He was holding his head and tail high and his ears forward. Then I saw his tail wag ever so slightly. I couldn't help myself. I responded. He took this as an encouragement and moved to investigate my personal places. Good manners, however, demanded that at the first pass, I play coy and leap sideways. After a little more ritual posturing, I let him satisfy his curiosity, and he let me investigate him. Just then, his master appeared at the end of the street. "Richelieu, come here!" What an elegant name, I thought.

Well, as soon as I got back to Hilton Park, the others smelled me, realized I'd been slumming—their term, not mine—and angrily chased me home. All but Reginald, that is. He just yawned and walked away.

When I went into the living room, Babette was on the phone talking to a friend. I heard her say she was going back to France—her marriage was on the rocks. I immediately panicked, convinced I'd be separated from my beloved Richelieu.

The next day, I hurried back to Colony Street and told him. He's a real cool cat, I mean a cool canine. He reacted calmly and rationally and told me not to worry—he'd think of something. Then, just before dinnertime, he had a brilliant idea. He'd make his master want to get rid of him and ingratiate himself to Babette. That sounded great, so we trotted back to my place together. I led him into the kitchen through the doggy door and shared my dish with him.

Babette was depressed that evening and was glad for company. She dished out more food, then let us lie down in front of the TV, while she spent the evening on the sofa sniffing and blotting her eyes. I would have jumped up and licked her face, but I figured it would be smart to have Richelieu do it. He agreed.

It wasn't until the next morning that Babette collected her wits enough to wonder to whom Richelieu belonged. She read his collar, then made a phone call. Shortly thereafter, his master appeared with a leash and dragged him home. Just before they left, Richelieu shot me a sly glance and wagged his tail to let me know he'd take care of things. He came back within the hour, and once more his master dragged him off.

Richelieu didn't come right back again, so I knew he'd been locked up. I went over and found the two of them in their backyard, the master trying to tempt him with tidbits. Richelieu was answering with angry growls and snapping at his fingers. Finally, the man gave up and went back inside. Richelieu came to the chain link fence, and we rubbed noses. He said everything was going according to plan.

Sure enough, after a week of visits on my part and more phone calls from Babette to Richelieu's master, he came over one afternoon with my love on a leash. He sat down with Babette, signed a paper, and left, completely befuddled as to what had come over his dog. Since then, Richelieu and I have been in dog heaven.

Then just yesterday, Babette took us both to the vet for shots and started packing her bags. I was wild with joy. We're going back to France, and Richelieu is going with us. No more of this stupid political correctness and conformism that kills all freedom of expression. I can hardly wait to get back where I can be loyal to my true self. Ah yes, *la belle France* where I can enjoy the privilege of hating everyone. Everyone, that is, except Babette and Richelieu.

# WHY ARE THEY ALWAYS SMILING?

IT was obvious to Jennifer that Solange—thirty-five, haughty, and attractive—wanted Americans to know she was French and respect her for it. Bitch, she thought, I'd rather be working with a mule. And the way she tries to make eye contact with men on the street, it's embarrassing.

Solange's heels clacked a self-assured beat on the sidewalk and her auburn hair bounced between her shoulders as they made their way along Rodeo Drive. Jennifer had trouble keeping up. In contrast to the casual appearance of most of the people they passed, Solange was dressed in the style she apparently considered appropriate for being seen in public—a chic beige skirt and jacket, silk blouse, and a brown-and-gold Balenciaga scarf. "I think I'm going to like it here. I just need to get used to you Americans."

Jennifer snorted. "That's for sure."

"But tell me; why are the people at the office so hostile? I've behaved correctly toward everyone. And that comment I overheard—something about frogs out of water...."

"Frankly, they find you stand-offish."

"I don't understand them."

"What's to understand?"

"For one thing, the smiles I get from people I don't even know."

"At least we don't stare at every man we pass."

"I'm not staring. French women simply want men to look at them. It's just a game, but a serious one, and it keeps us on our toes. You should try it. It's good for the morale."

Jennifer looked at her watch. "Three-ten. The meeting's in twenty minutes."

"We'll make it."

"I don't know. All this traffic—"

"Oh, look—the cologne I've been searching for."

"Solange, we don't have time."

"It'll only take a second. I feel naked without it."

Jennifer gritted her teeth and followed.

Fifteen minutes later they climbed into Solange's rented convertible. Jennifer glanced at her watch again—this was one time she was glad Solange was driving. Out on the boulevard, Solange pulled into the far right lane—the light was red.

Jennifer looked at her with surprise. "The office is to the left."

"So it is."

The light changed and Solange jammed the pedal to the floor. They took off in a screech of tires, turning left in front of the adjoining lanes. Jennifer sucked in her breath and pressed both hands against the dashboard. The other drivers slammed on their brakes and leaned on their horns. Solange answered with a gesture like the one Americans use to throw salt over their shoulder. "You know, Jennifer, your driving regulations are illogical; you should have a single priority-on-the-right rule like in France."

As soon as they entered the side street, there was a howl from a siren. Solange looked in the mirror and saw a patrol car. *Merde!* She stopped and reached for her cologne, gave her neck a quick spray, and restored it to her bag before the officer got to her window.

He leaned down and nodded. "Good afternoon, ladies. May I see your driver's license?"

"Yes, officer." She handed it to him with a caressing look.

He examined it. "French, eh? Welcome to Los Angeles. However, I'm going to have to give you a ticket."

"Oh please, I shall be more careful in the future."

"I'm sorry, ma'am, but you nearly caused an accident."

As he was writing, Solange's expression soured. When he'd finished, he handed her the ticket and license with a smile. "Have a nice day."

Once he was out of hearing, Solange shook her head. "*Salaud!* What a hypocrite. How could he smile and give me a ticket at the same time?"

"He wasn't angry; he was only doing his job."

It was three-fifty-five when they pulled into their building's basement garage, and it took them another five minutes to walk up to the lobby, wait for an elevator, and get to the twentieth floor. When they entered the meeting room, Chet Hendrickson, head of the Los Angeles office, stopped speaking and looked at them. Then he smiled. "For those who've been out of town, let me introduce Solange Bellanger from our home office in Paris."

The session lasted forty-five minutes. When it was over, Jennifer whispered, "Let's get out of here before he remembers we were late."

"But I haven't greeted everyone properly." She made the rounds with the perfunctory French handshake. Jennifer had no choice but to follow.

Just as they were leaving, Hendrickson called out. "Just a minute, Ms. Bellanger, Mrs. Cole, close the door please."

Jennifer gritted her teeth. Well, here it comes.

But Hendrickson didn't look angry at all. "Thank you. I just wanted to ask how you two are getting along."

The truth would have been a tactical mistake, so Jennifer answered, "Very well, thank you."

"I'm so glad. The reason I've asked you to work closely together is that our people in Paris want to learn American PR techniques. Just don't interfere with each other's accounts; I need to know who's doing what."

Jennifer let out her breath and thought, Home free! I was sure the axe was going to fall.

Hendrickson smiled again. "One more thing—before the meeting, I invited everyone for a barbecue a week from Sunday. I hope you both can come."

They promised to be there and left. Once in the hall, Solange said she needed a few minutes to herself. Relieved, Jennifer headed for her office.

The first thing she saw when she opened the door was a memo propped up against her pen holder. It looked urgent so she picked it up and read it. In a panic, she grabbed the phone and punched Harry Niemuth's extension.

"Oh God, Harry, can you come down right away?"

"What's wrong, sweetheart? You sound terrible."

"Seems I rubbed Charley Duquesne the wrong way and lost his account. When Hendrickson finds out, I'm really in for it."

"Okay, hang on, I'll be right down."

He was in her office in no time and took her in his arms. "Tell me what happened."

"We were going over the figures together, he was having trouble understanding, and I lost my temper. I swear I'm going to kill that woman."

"What are you talking about?"

"Solange Bellanger. She's driving me crazy with her French antics. You know me—I *never* lose my temper. What am I going to do?"

"Come on now, let's calm down. It'll turn out all right, you'll see."

They were still clinging to each other when two rapid

knocks came at the door and Solange walked in. They broke apart, and Niemuth left without a word.

Jennifer exploded. "Dammit, Solange, in this country, you don't barge in! A closed door means you knock and wait for an answer."

Solange shrugged it off. "Wouldn't it be more logical to turn the bolt if you don't want to be interrupted?" Then she took a closer look—there were tears in Jennifer's eyes. "Oh, my dear, what's the matter?"

"Here, look at this." She handed Solange the memo. "Mr. Hendrickson's going to crucify me."

"It can't be that bad. Come on, let's go downstairs for a drink. You'll feel better."

The barbecue party was just getting started when they arrived. Jennifer was still worried, but she managed to put on a good face.

They were greeted by a gracious lady in tennis attire. "Hello, Jennifer. And you must be Solange Bellanger. I'm Carol Hendrickson."

Solange took her hand. "Delighted to meet you, Mrs. Hendrickson."

"Please call me Carol. Here are your name tags." Solange looked puzzled. Carol smiled. "They save the trouble of formal introductions."

Solange looked around. "What a lovely place you have. This is the first California home I've been in."

The living room and kitchen were one spacious unit separated by only a counter. The back of the room was solid glass with sliding doors opening onto a patio, beyond which she could see a swimming pool, jacuzzi, a wide lawn, a putting green, and thick shrubbery and trees hiding their neighbors from view.

Carol beamed. "Why thank you. Now, why don't you two go join the others outside?"

Solange followed Jennifer out to the patio. She did a double-take when she saw Hendrickson tending the barbecue in short pants, Hawaiian shirt, white apron, and high chef's hat. His face lit up when he saw them. "Hello there. So glad you could come."

Solange held out her hand but withdrew it when he failed to notice. "I was so happy to meet your wife, Mr. Hendrickson. She's an absolutely charming person."

"Please call me Chet." He handed her a plate with a large roll and hamburger and another to Jennifer. "The rest is over there."

They thanked him and went to the buffet. Jennifer helped herself to a little of everything, while Solange took only some coleslaw and potato salad. There were also individual plates, each with half a cooked peach on a bed of cottage cheese and lettuce and a stripe of mayonnaise with a maraschino cherry on top. Solange stared. "What in the world is that?"

"A salad. Here, have a Coke."

They found an unoccupied garden table and sat down to eat. Jennifer picked up her hamburger with both hands, while Solange attacked her own with fork and knife—the knife in her right hand, the fork in her left.

Jennifer chuckled. "How quaint."

Presently Carol Hendrickson joined them. "How's everything?"

Solange nodded. "Lovely. And these french fries, they're superb. You are an *excellente cuisinière.*"

Carol laughed. "They're from McDonalds. But tell me, how do you like California?"

"The climate is marvelous, and last Sunday I visited the Norton Simon Museum to see the Degas sculptures. Have you seen them?"

"No, but have you been to Disneyland yet? That's an absolute must."

"There's so much to see here—it's bewildering. I'm sure you

felt the same when you and your husband visited Paris."

"Actually, we did just about everything—the Eiffel Tower, the Crazy Horse Saloon, the Folies Bergères, Versailles, the Galleries Lafayette...."

"Did you visit any museums?"

"Yes indeed, we spent over an hour in the Louvre. Listen, I'd better circulate. But before I leave, I wanted to tell you, Solange—may I call you Solange?" Solange nodded, and Carol continued. "Chet is so happy about the way you two are working together. Now I know this is supposed to be a secret, but I heard how you stepped in and saved the Duquesne account."

Jennifer looked bewildered. "The Duquesne account? But, but I thought...."

Carol took Solange's hand and patted it. "Oh my, I've let the cat out of the bag, haven't I? You see, I play golf with Gladys Duquesne every Thursday. She talks a lot, you know. She told me you spent all last Saturday getting Charley to reconsider."

Jennifer was dumbfounded. "I don't understand...."

Solange shrugged her shoulders. "I didn't have anything else to do so I phoned him Friday after work. He invited me to spend the day on his yacht with his family. They're very *sympatiques*."

Carol beamed. "We're so glad it worked out. Well, I'd better get going. We'll chat more later."

As Carol left, Jennifer looked into Solange's eyes. She was beginning to see a different person. "Oh thank you so much. You stuck your neck out for me. I don't know what to say. I feel so guilty."

"Guilty? What for?"

"For the way I've been treating you."

"On the contrary, you're the first one here who's been candid with me. That's a true mark of friendship."

"You know, Solange, I had a hard time figuring you out at first, but this weekend I stumbled on a marvelous book about the differences between the French and Americans. It's been an eye-opener."

"Oh?"

"Well, for example, Americans feel threatened when a Frenchman they're talking to brings his face too close. Our personal bubble is bigger."

"So *that's* why people keep backing off. I thought I had bad breath."

"Also, you have to reassure Americans with a smile that everything's all right. Otherwise we don't know where we stand."

"But a smile for no good reason means we are not taking the person seriously, or else we're flirting."

"Not in this country. Even businesses advertise how friendly they are."

"I guess you're right. And I've noticed something else—Americans don't like heated discussions. In France, we all talk at once, and we say what we think and feel. It's a game, like fencing. We don't take it personally."

Jennifer laughed. "You're practically quoting the book."

"Will you help me?"

"Of course. I have an idea; I want you to see Disneyland with me next weekend."

"But that's for children."

"Trust me."


They got to the park early enough to find good seats at the edge of an outdoor restaurant where they'd have a good view of the big parade.

Solange looked around. "You know, Jennifer, I never saw so many families together as happy and carefree. It's as if everybody knew one another. There's something in the air that's completely new to me."

"Listen. I hear the band."

As the bouncy strains of the "Mouseketeers March" became

louder, the crowd moved off the street onto the sidewalks. The parade came into view, and the excitement swelled. Mickey and Minnie Mouse, Snow White and the Seven Dwarfs, Pluto, Goofy, Dumbo, and other Disney characters passed by, dancing, waving, with huge smiles on their oversize heads.

The joy was so overwhelming that Solange had trouble keeping her composure. She felt like laughing and crying at the same time. "This is wonderful!" she said, "I think I'm beginning to understand. You know, Jennifer, we French are a happy people too—we just don't show it the same way. I think your country is marvelous, and I want to learn to get along. I'll even make an effort to smile more."

Jennifer took her hand. "Now don't go overboard; I like you just the way you are."

"Believe me, the feeling is mutual. And don't worry—I'm much too French to change. You know, Jennifer, our friendship will probably always be like France and the USA—rocky at times, but solid. We might squabble and criticize each other from time to time, but underneath, there will always be respect and affection. Just two things."

"Oh?

"Don't ever serve me a salad like the one we had at the Hendricksons' barbecue, and don't expect me to put ketchup on my french fries. *Quelle horreur!*"

# THE WATCH

THÉODORE Dumont studied the face of the attorney seated across the boardroom table. On the surface, the offer seemed like a good opportunity. However, something about the man disturbed him. Although he'd come to America with his parents as a child, Théodore still had a typical French mistrust of others. He reached into his pocket and cradled his watch in his palm until it felt warm. A feeling of confidence dispelled his remaining doubts. He stood up, shook his head, and smiled.

"Please thank your associates for their interest in our corporation, but it doesn't fit in with our plans. Good-bye. My assistant will show you out."

Dumont never wore a wrist watch of the elegance befitting a man of his wealth and power, but kept a cheap timepiece with large children's numbers in his pocket. The one he had at present was only the latest of a long line going back to the original dollar watch he'd been given when he was five. To his business associates, it was an enigma; to the media, an object of "human interest." But he avoided questions about it, and buying replacements as they wore out was a responsibility he never delegated. The fact was, he considered it his best friend, an alter ego, a mentor.

He never used it to tell time. Rather it was a reminder of a basic truth concerning human nature that the first one had revealed to him. Now, its mainspring long since broken and its gears rusted, it lay in a velvet-lined box at home in his wall safe, preserved in a revered state of arrested decay.

The lesson it had taught him was that no one, no matter how close, can be counted on to be completely candid and forthright in all circumstances, and that even the most well-intentioned and harmless deviation from the truth can have far-reaching consequences. It was not the thieves, the embezzlers, the con men, and the like who posed the greatest threat; it was the "nice guys" one had to watch out for. One had to learn to be one's own actor, claque, and critic.

On the other hand, the expedient little white lies that parents sometimes tell their children could, as in Théodore's case, turn out to be the most effective and useful object lessons in life.

The watch was not Théodore's only eccentricity. For three hundred and sixty-three days a year, he remained a tough and unapproachable industrial baron with one thing on his mind—extending his empire. But unlike most others, his successes were never obtained through dishonesty. He played his assets like chessmen and profited only from his superior skill and his adversaries' mistakes. Those he perceived to be cheating, he maneuvered into hoisting themselves on their own petards. By choice, he had no friends, no family, no ties of any kind.

However, on one special day, the day before Christmas, at the annual party he gave for his employees and their families, he underwent a metamorphosis. For that occasion, the largest meeting room in the corporation's headquarters was transformed into a lavish make-believe North Pole, with a corral full of live reindeer, life-size stuffed polar bears, the mythical toy workshop with animated elves, and a throne occupied by a jovial Santa in the person of Théodore Dumont himself.

The little children were brought up, one by one, to sit on his lap and tell him what they wanted for Christmas. A secretary sat by, noting the requests and passing them back to another employee, who kept a phone line to the department store open until they'd all been heard. No wish was refused.

After the ice cream, cake, and hour-long pageant, the wrapped gifts were brought in and distributed. The parents knew they were not to utter a word of thanks. This was between Théodore Dumont and the children. The only thing that mattered to him was the look of excitement and happiness on their faces. For the moment they were blessed with angelic innocence; they were Théodore's contact with Heaven. Soon, much too soon, they would learn the realities of life.

Théodore shook his head as he remembered how at the age of nine he had caught his father in a boldfaced lie. It happened that he'd been telling a friend's parents about a movie in which, at a crucial moment, a thousand Arab warriors had abandoned an attack because it was time to prostrate themselves in prayer toward Mecca. But he had used the word 'prostitute' instead of 'prostrate.' Humiliated by the gales of laughter that greeted his mistake, he'd resolved to get the two meanings straight once and for all and had stopped off at his father's house on his way home—this was something he couldn't ask his mother. He'd phrased his question, "Dad, what's 'prostitute' mean?" He remembered how, to his surprise, his father had been thrown off balance, casting about for an answer suitable for a nine-year-old. But Ted, like most children of his age, was a lot better informed than his parents suspected. He knew what a whore was—his only problem was vocabulary.

"Well, a prostitute is a lady who gets married but only for a short time."

Ted couldn't believe it. Out of curiosity he tightened the screw. "Exactly for how long, Dad?"

Ted watched in fascination as his father's eyes shifted and

his face got red. The answer, when it came out, was in a voice distorted with moral discomfort.

"Oh, for only a month or so."

Ted let it drop and turned away, amused and disappointed. But this wasn't the first time. The initial and most shocking disillusionment had come on his fifth Christmas, when his world had suddenly been turned upside down and he needed something solid to cling to.

His parents had divorced, and in a way, he felt it was his fault. Now, instead of the home he'd always known, with a mother, a father, a loving wet-tongued dog, all in the big warm house with the womb-like recesses he liked to play in, he was alone with his mother in a cold, almost bare dance studio on the third floor of a building above a J.C. Penney store. In his mind it all went back to the last time his mother had made him take his cod-liver oil, a morning ritual he'd come to anticipate with horror. This time he'd thrown a tantrum and screamed at his father, "I hate Mommy! I hate her! I want you to kill her!"

The couple argued over money, how she kept house, how he drove the car, how to bring up their child, what to feed the dog—all of which Théodore now understood were symptoms of a more fundamental incompatibility. His father, a war veteran a generation older than she, had a facial war wound that had left him disfigured and given to outbursts of exasperated rage. His mother, a beautiful and vivacious young woman, dazzled by his father's status as a war hero and by the prospect of emigrating to the USA, had given up a dancing career to marry him.

It was one of these crises that brought things to a head. It was late one night. Ted was upstairs asleep, Queenie's furry body stretched out beside him. Suddenly downstairs there were shouts. His parents were having a brawl, this one more violent than he'd ever heard. He got out of bed, opened his bedroom door and went to the top of the stairs. The sight that greeted his eyes sent him into a panic. His mother was on her back, his father astride her, holding both her wrists on the floor beside her head. Teddy screamed in terror. His father looked up; there was madness in his eyes. "So you wanted me to kill your mother. All right then!"

Teddy could no longer see anything through his tears. "Please, Daddy, don't do it! I didn't mean it!"

The boy's sudden appearance was enough to make his father relax his grip and for his mother to free one of her hands and sink her nails into his face. He scrambled to his feet, and from the floor she sent a heel smashing into his genitals. Now he was the one on the floor, writhing in pain, and she was running up the stairs toward Teddy.

He remembered her calling a taxi from the bedroom phone, tossing a few clothes and his Pooh Bear into a suitcase, and then dragging him out of the house past his moaning father. The details that followed were now very dim—days at the house of his mother's closest friend, a visit to a lawyer, a judge who asked him with whom he wanted to live....

Then came the dance studio with one of its two small dressing rooms converted into a make-do bedroom with two army-surplus cots, an old bureau, a small table, and two chairs. The tiny bathroom served also as their kitchen. Dishes were washed in the basin and stored on the back of the toilet, and their meals were cooked on a hot plate set on a sheet of plywood over the bathtub. It was winter and their perishables were kept in a box on the ledge outside the window. One night a cat knocked it over, and the next morning he saw his mother cry.

For the first few months they ate mostly meatloaf or soup and usually only an apple or cookies for dessert. After getting herself and Teddy settled, she'd had just enough money left over to have the floor of the large room sanded and polished and full-length mirrors and handrails installed. Too proud to accept help from his father, she gave ballet lessons to groups of clumsy housewives. As for Teddy, there was not much for him to do aside from coloring books and listening to the radio, and while his mother was busy, he had to remain alone and quiet in the bedroom.

But all was not bleak. Christmas was almost upon them. Everything joyfully signaled the approaching season—the gaudy animated displays in the store windows, the Santa Clauses ringing their bells on the street corners, the blinking Christmas trees, the bright green-and-red festoons stretching from pole to pole across the main street, the layer of fresh snow on the roofs....

"Mommy, will Santa Claus come see us like he did in the other house?"

"Of course he will, Teddy."

"Can we go see Santa like we did last year?"

"Yes, sweetheart, if you really want to."

The department store she took him to was Paradise. The lights and the music coming over the loudspeakers radiated warmth and promise, and the displays were dazzling. They went upstairs to the toy department and took their places at the end of a line of parents and children waiting to talk to Santa. Teddy squeezed his mother's hand. Down at the end, seated on a throne was a white-bearded Santa with a little girl on his lap. She kept her eyes bashfully lowered and giggled every time he said something to her. Finally he put her down and the next child took her place.

After twenty minutes, it was Teddy's turn, and he felt Santa's strong hands lifting him up to his knees. "Ho, ho, ho. My, you are a big boy. Have you been good this year?"

Teddy was too intimidated to say anything but managed to nod his head.

"Now, what would you like Santa to bring you this Christmas?"

This time a nod wouldn't be enough. Anyway Santa's lap and arm around him felt warm and comforting. He looked into his eyes and saw a daddy's kindness. He was no longer afraid.

"I wanna dog, anna airplane, anna truck, an crayons, anna

television. We don't have a television anymore."

"Ho, ho, ho. Well, you just keep being a good little boy and we'll see what we can do. Meeeerry Christmas." With that he put him down and gave him a fatherly pat on the cheek.

Teddy's world was bright again. His mother got a table-top Christmas tree and decorated it with a single strand of lights and walnuts wrapped in tinfoil and colored plastic. Teddy was a little disappointed but didn't say anything. He soon got over it and when he was put to bed on Christmas Eve, he fell asleep happy. Santa's reindeer and sled would soon be landing on the roof with a dog, an airplane, a truck, crayons and a new television set.

But the next morning when he sneaked out of bed and looked under the tree, there was nothing. In a panic he pounced on his sleeping mother. "Mommy, mommy! Santa didn't come! He didn't bring me my presents!"

She sat up with a start and wrapped her arms around him. "Teddy, Teddy, don't cry. There *is* a present for you. Come on, I'll show you."

She got up, led him back to the tree and pointed to a minuscule package. "There, see? Open it."

But Teddy stared at her in disbelief. It was too small. It couldn't be an airplane, or a truck, or a television.

But his mother insisted. "Open it, Teddy."

In a state of shock, he pulled on the ribbon, tore off the paper, opened the box and pulled out the present. It was a dollar watch. He looked up at his mother, searching for an explanation.

She knelt down, put both hands on his shoulders. "You're a big boy now, Teddy. You don't want baby's toys anymore, do you? Santa brought you this to help you grow up. This is a very important present. Now you can learn to tell time like grown-ups and do things when you're supposed to. What do you think about that?"

It happened that Teddy had heard an unpleasant rumor

somewhere but had rejected it as something he didn't want to know for sure. But now the moment of truth had been forced upon him and only his mother could put things straight.

"Mommy, is there a Santa Claus?"

Her face went blank, and he watched her eyes shifting from side to side.

# WATER FOR M'BOUKA

THE ancient Piper Cub bounced to a stop at the end of the Senegalese bush airstrip, spun around, and wobbled back to the shack that housed the field's facilities. Its lone passenger, Charles Lebec, peered through the window, mumbling, "Everything happens at once—the Colette thing, the water problem down here. What next? Now where the hell is Mass?"

As the engine coughed and died, he ran his comb through his hair, opened the door, and dropped to the ground, dragging his flight bag behind him. He pushed his sunglasses up on his forehead and scanned the black locals standing by in their long faded *boubous*. One of them came running. "Hey, it's me."

Charles did a double-take. He remembered Massaër only as a fellow student and friend in Paris. Seeing him in a *boubou* would take some getting used to.

Mass laughed and gave him a brotherly hug. "Hi, you handsome bastard. What have you been up to?"

"Same as always—running around the French countryside playing little Dutch boy."

"How do you like the job?"

"Keeps me on my toes."

"Hey, I'm sorry about Colette. What happened?"

"Well, she didn't like me being away so much. Wanted me to pull strings and get a desk job. That, of course, would have been bad for my career. Besides, I like to travel."

"That's it?"

"No, the actual breakup came one day while I was trying to do a little housekeeping. She flew into a rage and said she was fed up with what she called my obsession with neatness. Claimed she could never find anything after I straightened up the apartment. What is it with artists anyway? Why doesn't their love of beauty apply to the way they live?"

Mass nodded. "Come on."

Charles followed him to a bush taxi, an old Renault pickup with benches under a metal shell. Once Mass had exchanged a few words in Wolof with the driver, Charles asked, "So exactly why did you send for me?"

"Like I said in my letter, our water supply's in trouble. The Casamance region never had a shortage before, but now wells are drying up. I tried for months to get some expertise down here, but the imam—he's our priest—kept saying Allah will take care of everything. I finally talked the village chief into sending me to Dakar to get a subsidy to bring you in."

"Well, it works out fine for me. Maybe a little time and distance between me and Colette will make her realize what a good thing we had. And it'll give me a chance to get my head on straight. Paris was driving me up the walls. Everything kept reminding me of her—the apartment, the cafés, the shops, the streets. The worst was knowing she was somewhere out there almost within reach."

An hour later, they turned into a tree-shaded enclave consisting of a circular pavilion, corrugated metal sheds, a cement water tower, and a dozen whitewashed mud huts with straw roofs. Mass led Charles to one of them.

"This one is yours. The Rotary Club built all this as a stopover for tourists. It provides income for our village."

Charles pushed open the door. The furnishings were minimal—a cot under a mosquito net, a chair, a rickety wooden table, a propane lamp, a couple of shelves on the wall, and an electric bulb dangling from the ceiling—but everything was immaculate.

"This will do fine."

"Okay, the bathroom is the shed at the end of the path. The water's just one temperature—warm in summer, lukewarm in winter. It comes from the tank out back. Needless to say, use as little of it as you can. Everybody takes his turn at the pump. The propane lamp is for nighttime. There's no electricity after eleven. That blue spiral on the floor is a punk to keep the mosquitoes away. Here, I'll show you how to light it."

"Don't bother, I can figure it out."

"Listen, Charles, I have things to do. I'll be back for you in an hour. We're having dinner with the village chief, the imam, and a dowser."

"A dowser?"

"Yeah, I know, but play it cool, please."

Charles closed the door and swung his flight bag onto the cot. He proceeded to stow shirts, pants, Jockey shorts, and socks in meticulous piles on the shelves. Then he emptied the side pockets and carefully lined his toilet articles along the back of the table. The last object he pulled out was a framed picture of Colette. He sat down on the cot, brought it close to his face, and tried to impart life to it. Slim, twenty-five, long brown hair, a sexy smile. High strung, he thought, and with a short fuse, but the rest of the time a lovable companion. His mind went back to their tender evenings together listening to Mahler and sipping Martini & Rossi.

Mass eventually returned and led him to the pavilion. Three men came forward, the first a gentleman in his seventies with purple-black skin glistening in contrast to his white hair and gown. His regal bearing radiated wisdom and serenity.

Mass introduced him. "Charles, Khalifa Dala, our village chief." They shook hands.

The second was an ageless, spider-like little man wearing a look of distrust.

"This is Yorro Kano, our imam."

Charles held out his hand. Yorro only nodded.

Mass took Charles by the elbow and turned him toward the last of the three. "And I'd like you to meet our dowser, Abdou Tiongané."

Abdou, a thin, sleazy-looking individual in his thirties, who'd been studying Charles, offered him a limp handshake.

Chief Khalifa gestured toward the settee built against the waist-high outer wall. Charles sat down between Mass and Khalifa, with Abdou and Yorro at the ends. Two women in variegated *boubous* and turbans approached with chicken couscous, which they ladled out onto wooden plates. Mass slipped Charles a spoon.

While the fare was simple and the others ate with their fingers, there was a relaxed elegance about the dinner that commanded respect. Charles saw that, like the French, these people valued the art of conversation and considered it part of good dining. No one tried to hold forth. Instead, it was a nonstop witty exchange of thrusts and parries, mostly about the World Cup soccer matches they were following on the radio. What impressed Charles the most was the quality of their French. Their grammar and diction were impeccable. Aside from an unusual richness of voice and an intriguing touch of accent, they spoke no differently from educated Parisians.

When they'd finished, Khalifa cleared his throat. "Monsieur Lebec, we truly appreciate your coming. I must tell you, however, that the last expert the Government sent down shook everyone's faith in Western technology. He prescribed chemical fertilizers and pesticides without realizing how delicate our tropical vegetation is."

Yorro took over. "Which means you will have to respect the

traditions Allah gave us almost two thousand years ago. Abdou, our dowser, will advise you."

Charles was off balance, and it must have shown. Khalifa came to his rescue. "Monsieur Lebec, it's getting late. You must be tired, We'll talk again tomorrow."

Mass accompanied Charles back to his hut. Charles put his arm around Mass' shoulders. "Your imam doesn't seem overjoyed about my being here. What's the problem?"

"It's Africa's dilemma. We're at a crossroads. Right now, our only options are to save ourselves at the expense of our religion, or leave everything to Allah and wallow in misery."

"Isn't there a middle ground?"

"The imam doesn't think so."

"So what am I doing here?"

"Helping the chief and me do a tightwire act."

They stopped in front of Charles' hut. Mass put his hand on Charles' shoulder. "Don't let the Colette thing get you down. It'll work out."

"I sure hope you're right."

As soon as Mass left, Charles took down Colette's picture, straddled the chair, and gazed at it.

He was brought out of his reverie by a knock at the door. He opened and found the dowser looking around to make sure no one had seen him. They stared at each other for a long moment. When Charles recovered from his surprise, he stepped back and gestured toward the inside. "What can I do for you?"

Abdou came in but remained standing. "Can I speak just between us?"

"Of course."

"I thought maybe we could share what we know. You tell me what you figure out, and I'll check it out with my stick. That way, we'll be twice as sure."

Charles burst out laughing. "You're joking."

Abdou scowled. "I'm the one they'll believe, you know."

Charles hesitated, then nodded. "Yes, I guess you're right."

The next day, Mass took him on a walking tour of the village and the fields, where small children, each with a dog, sat in shelters guarding the crops.

"Pests?"

"Yes, monkeys."

"What do you grow?"

"Mostly peanuts."

"Those kids seem awfully young."

"The older ones are at school."

"Where are the men?"

"Taking it easy. The women do most of the work."

"You know, I like the way everything is so well organized here. There's only one thing I don't understand."

"What's that?"

"The people obviously like cleanliness. Your homes and the enclave are always spic and span. But what about all the abandoned vehicle carcasses along the roads, the piles of worn-out tires, plastic containers, dead batteries and other junk in the streets?"

Mass laughed. "I was waiting for you to say something about that. The fact is our trash was always degradable until you French came along. People here just don't know how to deal with cans, plastic, and the like, so nothing gets done."

The water problem hadn't yet reached the crisis stage, but it was getting there. They'd tried to deepen the wells, but the yield still wasn't sufficient. Charles got out his maps and went to work. For the first time since his arrival, he was doing something he liked. His morale improved, and his anguish over Colette decreased.

He finally decided the best place for a new well would be a thousand yards north of the village. Several days later, after an invocation by the imam, Abdou set out with his forked stick, with Charles, Mass, Khalifa, and Yorro following. When he reached the designated spot, his stick began to shake, then suddenly bent downward. Yorro raised both hands toward the heavens. *"Allah akbar!"* Mass shot Charles a sly wink.

They started digging, but nine days passed without results. Charles couldn't understand it. He went over his calculations several times. The results were always the same—this was the best place. Meanwhile, Abdou was becoming hostile. Only Mass showed any confidence. "Cheer up, friend, you'll hit water."

His prophesy came true a week later in the middle of a sweltering afternoon. Charles was resting under a kapok tree when a shout of triumph rang out from the well. He rushed over, looked down, and let out a whoop of joy at the agitated reflection of the sky on the gurgling brown water below.

That evening when he took down Colette's picture, he felt that something had changed. He wondered if it was the picture or the way he was perceiving it. He studied it more closely. Then it became clear.

Of course, he thought, she'd been knocking everything I believe in. Boy, love can sure mess up your mind. Dammit, I'm proud of what I do and how I do it. I'm my own person—good habits, bad habits, whatever. I made allowances for her, why couldn't she have made some for me?

At daybreak, he began assembling the two-cycle gasoline pump and galvanized pipe he'd ordered. Eventually, several villagers came by to watch. The imam was among them, but after only a minute, he snorted disdainfully and walked away. The others hung around a while longer, the men laughing and jabbering in Wolof, the women watching in silence.

Charles went to bed happy that night, but when he returned the following morning, he was dumbstruck. The equipment had disappeared. He exploded. "That goddamned imam!"

He rushed into the village and found Yorro chatting with several men. They froze when they saw him. He wanted to grab Yorro by the neck and shake him until his brains rattled, but he managed to control himself. He asked what he'd done with the pump. Yorro stared at him, and Charles realized he hadn't any idea what he was talking about. When he explained, Yorro extended both palms towards the sky. *"Incha Allah!"*

On the way back, a hunch prompted Charles to look into the well. Sure enough, sections of pipe were sticking up in the water, the pump obviously at the bottom.

It took him the rest of that day and all of the next to retrieve, flush, clean, and reassemble everything.

Frustrated, he needed to talk to someone. Mass wasn't around, so he went to the village chief and told him what had happened.

Khalifa shook his head. "No, it wasn't the imam, it was the women."

"The women?"

"Of course. The pump was a threat to their status. They not only bear and bring up children, they haul wood, pound millet, draw water, and keep house. They're very proud and protective of their role."

"But if we stay with the rope and bucket, they won't have time for anything else."

"You'll just have to find a way they'll accept."

Charles thanked him and returned to the well. The pump, pipe, fittings, and tools had once more been carted away. Yeah, he thought, I should have expected it.

When Mass finally showed up, they discussed the problem. Mass scratched his head. "Isn't there a better way the women could draw water than with a rope and bucket, maybe with a crank?"

"A windlass. Yeah, I thought of that, but it would be too slow."

Mass chuckled. "Too bad we can't hitch monkeys to a crank."

Then it hit him. "Would women accept animal power?"

"I suppose so, as long as they were made responsible for them."

"Then that's it—a bucket chain, geared to a windlass, and turned by a donkey."

This time, he asked Khalifa to get the village women's approval. Several days later, he got it and dove into his work. For the first time since leaving Paris, he hardly thought about Colette.

When the contraption was completed and they started it up, Mass watched in admiration. "I've got to hand it to you, Charles. That flow should take care of our needs for years."

Charles looked around. The women were smiling now.

The evening before Charles' departure, the village organized a feast in his honor. While waiting for Mass to pick him up, he opened his flight bag and started packing. He'd just inserted his neatly folded shirts into a paper bag and was maneuvering the pile of shorts into another when he stopped short. At least she was right about one thing, he thought, and with a sweep of his arm, he sent his toilet articles flying pell-mell into his flight bag. There was a knock at the door.

"Come in, Mass. Sit down."

Mass glanced at Charles' open flight bag and suppressed a smile. "Let's go. Everybody's waiting."

After a sumptuous banquet of baked fish, rice, yams, and tomatoes, followed by a fruit salad of bananas, pineapples and oranges, they unveiled a parting gift—the pump, fittings, pipe, and his tools, all cleaned and shiny new. Charles grinned at the women, shrugged his shoulders, and raised both palms toward the sky. There was a round of applause and laughter.

Then Mass produced a champagne bottle and glasses. Charles was nonplussed—alcohol was taboo among Muslims. He was even more astonished when Mass poured not only for the two of them, but for Khalifa, Abdou, and Yorro as well. And it was the village chief who proposed the toast. "My friend, *our* friend, we are grateful. Allah be with you."

Charles was overwhelmed, but as he looked through his

raised glass, he noted with dismay that it had none of its usual color and bubbles. Must be the long trip from France, he thought. Oh well, it's the gesture that counts.

As he brought his glass to his lips, he hardly noticed everyone was awaiting his reaction. He took a sip. "Water!"

Gales of laughter rang out. Even the imam had a smile. When it finally died out, Mass spoke up. "Charles, this may not be Piper-Heidsieck, but it's more precious to us than champagne is to the French. We offer you our thanks and wish you Godspeed." While everyone was applauding, Charles clinked glasses with Mass and murmured, "I'm the one who's grateful—this job has turned my life around."

"So you've decided how to handle the Colette problem?"

Charles winked. "Who's Colette?"

# TEDDY BEARS

"FRENCHIE has a teddy bear! Frenchie has a teddy bear!"

The mocking singsong brought tears to the eyes of six-year-old Pierre and made him hug the stuffed animal even tighter. He'd kept *Noo-Noorse* a secret until now, but he had felt especially lonely this morning, and so had brought his best friend to school with him.

Keith, the class bully, tugged at one of its legs. "Give me that. Only babies have teddy bears."

"It's *not* mine. I found it."

"It *is* yours. You're hugging it."

A seam split open, and Pierre cried out. In a desperate surge of strength, he wrested it from Keith's grip. He ran to the school's front steps, grasped it by its hind legs, raised it in the air, and bashed its head on the cement. "I hate you! I hate you!" On the second swing, sawdust flew out like a jet stream and settled on his hair and shoulders. A plastic eye fell on a step, vibrated to a stop, and stared up at him. He gasped.

The school bell rang, and with a shout the other children crowded pell-mell through the door, leaving him in the middle of a film of sawdust on the steps, a broken plastic snout, eyes, and *Noo-Noorse*'s shapeless velvet cover draped over a step like a Dali watch. He gathered up the pieces and eased them into his school pack. "Oh, *Noo-Noorse*, I'm sorry!"

It was only at dinner that his mother realized something was wrong. "Why aren't you eating?" He burst out crying, ran to his room, and threw himself on the bed. She followed and took him in her arms. "Oh, *mon petit chou*, what is it? Has Keith Lindley been mean to you again?"

He refused to answer. "*Maman*, I want my *papa*."

She shook her head and wiped away a tear. "Pierre, please try to understand. Your father is in Heaven now—we won't see him again until God calls us too. Now, come back to the table and finish your dinner. You want to be as big and strong as he was, don't you?"

He obeyed and tried to be brave, but when he'd been tucked into bed and his mother had kissed him and closed the door, he burst into tears again. In the middle of the night, he got up and attempted to bring his *Noo-Noorse* back to life by stuffing its body with socks and trying to get its plastic nose and eyes to stay on. Nothing worked.

The next day, his schoolmates ignored him. He felt more isolated than ever.

At dinner that evening, he brooded before his untouched plate. Suddenly he jumped up and ran around the table into his mother's arms. "*Maman*, I hate that school, I hate it! I don't want to go there anymore!"

"Don't cry, *chéri*. I have some good news. First, Mister Greystone, downstairs, is fixing *Noo-Noorse*—you'll have him back tomorrow. But the best thing is that as soon as school is over, you and I are going back to France. I'm going to teach in Neuilly, and you will be with French children again. We only have to stay here a few more weeks, so please be brave, all right?"

As soon as they landed in Paris, they took the train to Sables-d'Olonne, where Pierre's grandparents had a summer cottage right on the beach. There were other children to play with, and when they discovered he'd been in America, he became a local hero. They wanted to know if he'd ever seen a real cowboy, if he'd been to the top of a New York skyscraper, if he belonged to a street gang....

When vacation was over, his mother enrolled him in her school. He was happy now, and *Noo-Noorse* was relegated to the bottom drawer of his mother's armoire.

The morning routine at the *Ecole Saint-Eustache* included a break in the school's courtyard under the lax supervision of Father Benoit. It was a time for the children to let off pent-up energy in a chaos of shouting, laughing, running around, shoving, and playing with a soccer ball.

There was one boy, however, from another class, who always sat alone and sad on the stone step in front of the concierge's door. Like the others, Pierre was too involved in his play to pay any attention to him. Then one afternoon as he and his mother were leaving for home, they passed by the boy and his mother. They were speaking English with an American accent. Pierre wanted to stop, but his mother was in a hurry.

The next morning at recess, Pierre went over to him and said in English, "Hello, my name is Pierre. What is yours?"

The boy looked at him suspiciously before responding. Even then, he was reluctant. "Bradford. You speak English?"

"Yes. Do you want me to teach you to play soccer?"

"No, soccer sucks. I like baseball."

"I went to school in Boston last year. Where do you live?"

"Washington. My father's company made him come here to work for a while."

"You like our school?"

Bradford sneered. "I hate it. I hate everybody here. I wish we could go back home."

"Don't you know any French?"

"Some, but everybody makes fun of me."

Pierre looked into his eyes. His experiences in America came crashing back into his memory. "Where are you living now?"

"On Boulevard Bourdon, right by the river."

"I know where that is—we live real close to there. Do your parents let you go over to the Isle de la Grande Jatte?"

"What's that?"

"The island in the middle of the Seine right across from where you live."

"They don't let me go anywhere. Mom says it isn't safe for me to play outside by myself."

The following day, Pierre got his mother to stop and talk to Brad and his mom.

Her name was Melissa. She seemed pleased to hear English. "How do you do. Brad just told me about you and your boy. I'm so glad Brad's finally found someone to talk too. He feels lost here. He just doesn't have an ear for languages. Say, maybe the two of them could visit sometime outside of school. What do you think?"

"Of course. Anytime."

"What about Sunday? Pierre could come to our apartment for lunch and they could spend the afternoon together."

"No problem. Give me your address and I'll drop him off."

As they parted, Pierre turned around and waved. For the first time, Brad wore a happy grin.

While they were waiting for Melissa to call them to lunch, Brad asked, "You wanna see my room?"

"Sure."

Brad led him down the hall and opened the door. Pierre followed him in and looked around. The walls were covered with pictures of all kinds of airplanes, and toy models adorned the windowsills and furniture.

Then his eyes lighted on the bed. He was startled to see an oversize brown teddy bear resting against the bolster. He looked at Brad in surprise, at the stuffed animal again, then back at Brad.

The boy looked mortified. He was struggling to find an excuse. Finally, he thought of something. "That *was* mine when I was a baby. I don't like it anymore, but my mom does. She keeps it on my bed.

Pierre smiled sadly. "I had one too, only smaller. It was my best friend. I used to take it to bed with me every night."

"Please don't tell anybody at school. Okay?"

"No, I won't. Anyway, I bet they all have a secret one of their own at home."

Brad looked relieved. Pierre picked up the teddy bear and gave it a hug.

# THE IMPORTANCE OF
# NOT BEING ERNEST

WHEN Jean-Marie Bascombe walked into my office, my mouth dropped open. He looked like an Ernest Hemingway clone—square jaw, white hair, mustache and beard, safari jacket, even a stogie sticking out of his mouth.

Furthermore, he didn't sound the least bit French. In fact, he'd cultivated an authentic folksy American style of speaking. He let me know immediately I was to call him Bascom, not Bascombe, and no first name.

I agreed to be his broker. What we had in common was that at fifty, we were both stuck in the wrong professions. He'd immigrated to the United States to teach French literature at our local university but was frustrated with the futility of trying to drum culture into "California yahoos."

It was our differences, more than anything else, that drew us together. He saw me as a person who accepted my status stoically, while I admired him as a free thinker.

A colleague of his gave me the details. "He travels a lot. For research, he says, but I'm sure he's just chasing his Hemingway fantasy. Bascom has traced every step he ever took in Europe. Last year he went to Key West to find people who'd known him. Now he wants to buy a place in Idaho, another Hemingway haunt. He's even written a novel."

Just before his summer vacation, Bascom invited me to his apartment for a drink. As I got there, a young lady was leaving. Both were glum. He let me in, disappeared into the kitchen, and returned with two triple shots of scotch. He sat down and stared at the rug. "Should have been a monk." I understood—a sexual fiasco.

I soon realized he had a tragic flaw—a self-destruct mechanism that aborted everything he started. His flamenco guitar playing was a good example. He'd taken it up as an attribute of his Hemingway image, the closest analogy he could find to bullfighting. When he attacked the first notes, the effect was dazzling. He'd begin with descending chords played with passionate rasgados, followed by frenetic arpeggios, headlong flights up and down Moorish scales, and culminating in a dramatic rallentando as if to announce the imminent fate of mankind. But nothing ever followed. Never a statement of theme, never a melody, only the introduction.

"It's all my father's fault." He drained his glass and got up. "Here, you need a refill." He was back in a minute.

"I loved that man." He sighed. "Well, cheers." Another long silence. "You want the truth? I hated the sonovabitch. Always felt we were in a footrace. Thought I'd be free after he died, but he's still there, watching, needling."

"You've done all right."

"Naaa, could've been a Hemingway scholar instead of a dead-end assistant professor of French. They won't advance me because I don't publish. If they only knew how I loathe Proust. But Hem, there was a man for you."

"What's the matter with Proust?"

"A pip-squeak who couldn't end a sentence."

He picked up his guitar and launched into one of his frenzied introductions. His cigar rolled off the edge of the coffee table. I picked it up and listened.

He gave up with an "Aw, the hell with it," and sank into a reverie. After another round of drinks, he picked up the guitar again. I watched his fingers race over the strings until the music faded from my consciousness. When I woke up, he was snoring.

I didn't hear from him again until September, when he phoned to say he had something special to show me. As soon as I got there, he guided me to a rack on the wall cradling a shiny new rifle with a telescopic sight.

"What's so special about it?" I asked.

"That's a custom-built three-thirty-eight caliber Win. mag. with Sako action, a Douglass air-gauge premier grade sporter weight barrel and a three-to-nine-power Leopold duplex scope. Which is to a hunter what a Ferrari is to a car buff. Run your hand over the stock, George. Doesn't that feel like Cleopatra's thigh?"

"If you say so."

"That's a Reinhart-Fajan stock made from a special grade of Bastogne walnut."

"What are you going to do with it?"

"Hunt, what else? Flying back to Idaho over Thanksgiving. Found a cabin. The real estate agent is taking me hunting where Papa Hemingway used to go. Going to get me a deer head of my own to replace the one on the wall. That one, I bought. This one will be legitimate."

I phoned the night he got back. No answer. I finally reached him Monday evening. He said to come over. He sounded troubled.

When I arrived, he'd already consumed more booze than usual. He didn't look in the mood to talk, so I waited. Finally, I asked about the cabin.

"Yeah, I bought it. Needs work. It'll keep me busy when I'm not skiing or fishing." Then through clenched teeth, "I'm sure as hell never going hunting again."

"Come again?"

Anguish distorted his face. "It was awful. Went looking for deer with this guy Buzz. We got separated. I stumbled on a giant buck grazing at the edge of a meadow—beautiful, noble. What a sensation. Then I pulled the trigger."

He covered his face with both hands. "The bullet slammed him against a tree. I went over and nearly passed out. Raw meat, broken bones, blood. Then our eyes met." Tears welled up. "Should have put him out of his misery. Instead, I panicked and ran." He shook his head and wailed, "How the hell could he do it?"

"How could who do what?"

"Hemingway. Kill for the fun of it." He shook his head. "I loved that bastard. Now I can't get him out of my system. He's going do me in one of these days."

Eventually, he did begin to talk about Idaho again—skiing, fishing, writing—but not a word about hunting. He kept his guns and knives, but the deer head disappeared.

Then one evening, he said he had encouraging news. "Think I found an agent for my novel."

When we'd drained our glasses, I followed him into the kitchen. He balanced his cigar on the edge of the table and went to work on the second round.

Suddenly I sniffed. "I smell smoke."

"So do I. Shit, the wastebasket's on fire."

He picked up a saucepan of soup and dashed it on the flames. "Damned cigar. Must have rolled off the table."

Before I left, he invited me to accompany him and a group of graduate students on a weekend hike in the Sierras.

Two weeks later, we were at the trail head of Army Pass. To hurry the others along, he and I put on our backpacks and waited where they could see us. Presently, a California beach-type blonde called Peggy McPhearson joined us and asked him if she could hike with him. He winked at me and said he'd be delighted.

By two, we'd made it to our campground. While most of the students went for a swim in a nearby lake, she sat on a log brushing her long blond hair. If Bascom noticed, he didn't let on.

After dinner, we settled around the campfire, Peggy between Bascom and me. During a lull, she mumbled something about her worn-out sleeping bag.

He chuckled. "I throw off so much heat, if you're anywhere near my tent, you'll be plenty warm."

People began to yawn and leave. I got up and went behind a tree. On the way back, I noticed her hiking boots in front of his tent. He was gazing at the embers. I whispered, "Congratulations, you have a house guest."

"What are you talking about?"

"Peggy."

"I'll be damned."

The next morning, she seemed happy, but he was subdued. Another fiasco? I wondered. Sure enough, later in the day, he confirmed it.

When we got back to town, he invited me up for a drink. After two triple shots, his morale picked up. He told me Peggy had attributed his failure to the altitude and said she'd see him Thursday.

On the appointed evening, my phone rang. It was he.

"George, listen. I've had a little, uh…accident. Can you help me get home?"

"Where are you?"

"University Hospital."

I got there fast. The receptionist asked me to see a Doctor Morelli first.

"Mister Shilling, your friend has four stab wounds in his left thigh. When the police found him, he was unconscious.

From the angle of the penetrations, it's clear the wounds were self-inflicted. But that's not the most serious thing. Were you aware he's an alcoholic?"

"I've never seen him drunk."

"That's not the criterion. He needs treatment."

Bascom let a nurse help him into my car, but when we got to his apartment, he shook me off. "Thanks, just wanted your company."

He got the door open, eased himself down, and propped his leg up on the coffee table. "Get me a drink, okay? Damned hospital is dryer than the Sahara."

This wasn't the moment to quibble. I fixed us both a scotch, then sat down and waited.

"Yes, I want to talk about it." He took a long drink and stared at his bandaged leg. "I'm no good as a man. Peggy came over this afternoon. Slim, satin skin, green eyes, the body of an angel. I wanted her. But I wilted. She tried to help. 'No problem,' she said, 'it can happen to everyone.' Bullshit! It *always* happens to me.

"After she left, I blew my stack. I stabbed myself four times before the pain registered. When I saw the blood, I had a vision of the deer I shot and passed out. Peggy must have come back."

He sighed. "I wish I could relive my college days. There was this gal named Cindy. Everything was great until one of my friends said she reminded him of my mother. I took a closer look. He was right—there *was* a resemblance. That's when I began having problems. Now this. Must have been the booze."

"Bascom, you ought to cut down."

"Bullshit. Booze kills the pain of life. Except for a few friends, humanity turns my stomach. If I had my finger on the doomsday button, I'd obliterate the whole mess.

"At least when I was young, I had illusions." He sighed again. "Now look at me. What do I have to look forward to? A cabin in Idaho. Yeah, that's an illusion too, but what else do I have? I can't even tell if I'm French or American."

Another long silence.

"You want to hear the supreme irony? We're supposed to spend our lives striving for wisdom, right? Well, that's mistake numero uno, because wisdom is the first toll of the bell. It destroys illusions and inhibits the commission of follies, the very essence of life. Chew on that for a while."

The following summer, I went to Idaho to spend my vacation with him. When I turned onto the dirt road to his cabin, he was talking to someone on his front porch. He gave me a brotherly abrazo. "Damned glad to see you, old buddy. I'd like you to meet Sheriff Caldwell."

The man was the embodiment of the old west—tall, lanky, the friendly, weather-beaten face of an old bloodhound, and wearing a ten-gallon Stetson. He held out a huge paw. "Welcome to Idaho, mister."

I was about to rest my butt on the aspen railing, when Bascom grabbed my arm. "Don't sit on that. Needs fixing."

Caldwell drained his glass. "Bascom, I gotta go. Glad to meet you, mister." He left, and Bascom disappeared into the cabin.

I looked around. The porch furniture—oversize rustic—consisted of armchairs with leather cushions and a table, on which was an empty highball glass, a massive ceramic ashtray with squashed-out cigar butts, and an open copy of *Death in the Afternoon*. A minute later, he was back, one glass already to his lips, another held out to me. I looked him over. He had on a pair of short pants of the same twill as his safari jacket, just like Hemingway's picture on the book jacket. He saw me looking at his scars. "Hell, Hem had scars too."

"Any news about your novel?" I asked.

"Sort of. Tell you later."

We spent a pleasant month together, working on the cabin. At the end of the day, we'd sit and drink on his porch talking and watching the sun go down.

•

Later that fall, he announced he was in love, again with a graduate student. The consummation of their relationship, he said, was at hand.

Two days later at eleven in the evening, my phone rang. It wasn't the voice I expected. "This is Doctor Morelli. I think you'd better get here as soon as you can."

"What is it?"

"It's your friend Bascom again. He's shot himself."

"Oh, my god. Is he dead?"

"No, but I think he's trying to castrate himself. He shot himself in the left thigh.'

"Was he alone?"

"No, there was a young lady. She was in the bathroom when it happened. It's a good thing she's cool-headed. She put a tourniquet around the leg and called the paramedics."

They released him from the hospital a week later, and I drove him home. He winced as he struggled out of the car. All he let me do was hand him his crutches. As soon as we got upstairs, he proceeded to make drinks.

"I thought you were going to cut down, Bascom."

"I need this. It's all I have left. Besides, Papa Hem said a man doesn't exist unless he drinks."

"What about your novel?"

"Didn't I tell you? All the agents I sent it to hated it."

"I don't want you dead, Bascom. Why don't you get rid of your guns?"

"Never intended to kill myself, George. Just wanted to get rid of two traitors. Don't worry, I've renounced all truck with women." He mused for a few seconds. "It all began with my mother."

"Your mother?"

"Yeah, I know. Never told you about her. Truth is, I was an unwanted child. She said God had burdened her with me as a punishment for her sins. She'd screwed my father before they were married. She convinced me I was no goddamn good, and he made me believe the only way to save my soul was to outdo Superman. Now you know why I don't want to be called Jean-Marie. Jean was my father's first name, Marie was hers. I came to this country mostly to get away from them."

Sometime later, Peggy McPhearson came downtown looking for me. "It's about Bascom. I'm sure he told you I was the cause of his first accident."

"It wasn't your fault."

"I know. I wanted to ask if you could do anything so he'd let me see him once in a while."

"Why not phone him?"

"I have, but he's afraid of me."

"Maybe you should leave him alone."

"But I just want to talk to him."

Her voice had become sad like a little girl's. I looked at her in surprise. She shook her head, and her eyes filled with tears. "I love Bascom. He doesn't have to take me to bed."

She broke into sobs, then wiped her eyes and blew her nose. "Will you talk to him?"

"Of course."

I went to see him after work. "I, uh.... McPhearson dropped in this afternoon. Why don't the three of us get together sometime?"

"Rotten idea."

"Come on, Bascom, I'm asking you as a friend."

"Oh, all right, if you really want to."

The following week an opportunity presented itself—a chamber music concert. Peggy sat between us. Bascom was so enthralled with the music he couldn't stop talking about it.

No sooner had I returned to my apartment than the phone rang. It was Peggy. "Thank you so much, George. When can we get together again? I'm afraid to take the initiative."

"Okay, I'll try."

Bascom phoned a week later and invited me for lunch on campus. I called Peggy and suggested she 'just happen' to spot us. The ruse worked, and the three of us started doing things together. Bascom relaxed, and she took on the glow of a woman in love.

Meanwhile, I'd agreed to take a two-day mule trip down the Grand Canyon with him—he couldn't hike anymore because of his leg. Peggy picked up on it. "Could I come along? Please?"

Bascom turned his palms upward and shrugged in a "why not?" gesture. Peggy clapped her hands.

The trip was a disaster. The Kaibab trail is steep, in places carved out of the canyon wall. When the mules stop and gaze into the abyss, their hoofs only centimeters from the edge, all you can see over their heads is the bottom, thousands of feet down. Bascom froze.

The atmosphere on the way home was morbid. When we arrived, he said he didn't want to see anybody for a while.

I waited until Christmas before trying to reach him, but he'd left for Idaho. Meanwhile, Peggy signed up for a seminar on Hemingway, to understand Bascom better, she said.

In mid-April, I got a worried call from Idaho. It was Sheriff Caldwell. "Could you come up here for a few days? We could use your help."

"What's the matter? Is Bascom all right?"

"I don't rightly know. Usually, when he gets into town, he shows up at the bar where us regulars congregate. This time, it was a couple of weeks before we knew he was around. I just happened to bump into him at the supermarket. When I asked him how he was, all he answered was 'Grim!' I figured I'd better leave him alone till he felt more sociable. But time went by and we all got worried, so last week I thought I'd mosey up to his place and check up on him. Problem is, I hadn't got half way up his road when he made me back off with a shotgun blast."

Next morning, I flew to Ketchum and rented a car. No sooner had I turned onto Bascom's property than the vehicle was splattered with dirt plowed up from the road by a carefully aimed shot.

I got out so he could see me. He picked up his field glasses, pointed them toward me, then waved for me to proceed. When I got close enough to see him clearly, I gasped. His face was drawn and pale, his eyes bloodshot, and he had a pronounced tic.

"What's going on, Bascom?"

"Look, amigo, don't take this personally. I just need to be alone."

"Hey, it's me. What do you think friends are for?"

"George, this is something I've got to work out myself."

I looked into his eyes. Aside from the tic, his face was a blank. I turned and walked back to my car.

He called out weakly, "Tell you what; I've chartered a plane to take pictures of the place from the air. Come along if you like. Eight-thirty at the Ketchum airport."

I got there early and introduced myself to Roy Hendricks, the pilot.

Just then, another pilot came in. "Can you do something about the guy out there with the white beard?"

"What's the problem?"

"I was taxiing out to the runway, when this nut starts walking across my path."

"Where is he now?"

"Still there. Come to the window."

I went over and looked. "Oh my God, it's Bascom." We ran out and I grabbed Bascom's arm. "What the hell are you doing?"

He looked at me with a dull expression. "Nothing. I wasn't paying attention. You ready, Roy?"

"Yeah, I'm ready. Where's your camera?"

"Oh yeah, the camera." He limped off and was back in a minute.

It didn't take long to get over Bascom's place. Roy began circling. "Altitude, five hundred feet, okay?"

Bascom shook his head. "No, higher."

I wondered why he was staring out the window instead of looking through his finder. Roy took us up another five hundred feet. "High enough?"

"Hell no." Roy turned in his seat, looked back at me for an explanation. I turned up empty palms. By the time Roy leveled out again, the cabin was a mere speck. He glanced at Bascom and growled, "Bascom, put your seat belt back on."

Without any warning, Bascom unlatched the door and lunged against it. The airsteam held it shut. I grabbed him, and Roy went into a steep left bank. Bascom went limp and began wailing incoherently. As soon as we landed, Roy ran around to Bascom's side and pulled him out. "If I see you around here again, I'll have Caldwell throw you in the cooler. Now get outta here."

Bascom sulked off toward his car. Roy calmed down a bit, and I asked him if he'd follow us to Bascom's place and bring me back down. "I don't think I should let him drive." He agreed, and I caught up with Bascom. On the way, I tried to talk to him, but he remained morose. "Bascom, how about if I stay with you for a few days?"

"I need to be alone, George. I'll be all right."

I knew arguing wouldn't do any good, so I went back to Ketchum and phoned Peggy. "Listen, Bascom's cracking up. He threw a couple of bad scares into us today."

"Oh? How?"

"Well, he wandered in front of an airplane and nearly got himself shredded by the propeller. Then we flew over his place to get some pictures and he tried to jump out."

Peggy gasped. "Oh my God! George, have you read Hemingway's biography?"

"No, why?"

"Hemingway tried to kill himself both of those ways."

"I didn't realize." Then I remembered. My heart sank. "Oh no! Hemingway shot himself, didn't he?"

"George, I'm dropping everything. I'll be there tomorrow."

As soon as she hung up, I rushed over to Sheriff Caldwell's office. He was on the phone. "Yeah, I'm leavin right now." He hung up and looked at me with an expression bordering on panic. "Roy Hendricks just flew over Bascom's cabin to check on him. Smoke is comin out from under the eaves. A fire truck is on its way. Come on, let's go."

He turned on the siren, and we screeched through town, laying rubber. When we pulled up to the cabin, two firemen were lowering an unconscious Bascom onto a tarpaulin and another was dragging out a smoldering mattress. A medic kneeled over him and went to work. Eventually, he looked up and shook his head. "Smoke inhalation." After they'd zipped him into a body bag, we entered the cabin. The firemen had aired it out.

The fire chief was inside. "We found him on his bed, clothed except for his right foot. A shotgun was beside him with the butt end next to his feet. Judging from what's left in that bottle, I'd say he passed out and his cigar ignited the mattress."

Caldwell shook his head sadly. "Sure looks like he intended to blow his brains out like Hemingway but couldn't bring himself to do it. And look at those darts."

Bascom had been throwing them at Hemingway's picture on the wall. Two were sticking in the frame, three were on the floor, and two were on the chair by the bed. Only one had hit the picture. It was sticking in Hemingway's nose.

When Peggy arrived, she came into my arms and broke into sobs. "I should have seen it coming."

We had him buried in the same cemetery as Hemingway. Our trip home was a sad one, and the advent of spring had none of its usual luster. A will was found, leaving everything to me, so I decided to spend my summer vacation finishing the work on the cabin—a sort of tribute.

One day, a letter arrived from an agent, saying he'd just received an answer from Randolph Press; they wanted to publish Bascom's novel. I phoned Peggy immediately.

There was a long silence before she answered. "How unfair! It would have changed everything." She asked if she could come to Idaho with me. I agreed and we flew up together.

Work on Bascom's cabin progressed rapidly. Each time we went into town, Sheriff Caldwell asked how it was going, so one day, I invited him up.

He appeared the following afternoon. "I sure have to hand it to you. Bascom would be pleased."

As the days were getting shorter and the sunsets more spectacular, I suggested we open a bottle and enjoy the view. I prepared drinks, raised my glass, then sat down on the aspen railing.

Suddenly there was a loud crack and I fell backward into the bushes. Peggy cried out and rushed down the steps, the sheriff right behind.

"George, George! Are you hurt?"

"I thought I'd fixed the damned thing."

Caldwell pulled me out and grinned. "You probably did, but Bascom unfixed it again. I'll bet he was tryin to tell you somethin."